ROMEO, JULIET & JIM

LARRY SCHWARZ &
IVA-MARIE PALMER

ROMEO, JULIET & JIM

Christy Ottaviano Books

HENRY HOLT AND COMPANY
NEW YORK

Henry Holt and Company
Publishers since 1866
175 Fifth Avenue
New York, New York 10010
fiercereads.com

Henry Holt® is a registered trademark of Macmillan Publishing Group, LLC.

Library of Congress Cataloging-in-Publication Data

Names: Schwarz, Larry, author. | Palmer, Iva-Marie, author.
Title: Romeo, Juliet & Jim : Book 1 / Larry Schwarz and Iva-Marie Palmer.
Description: First edition. | New York : Henry Holt and Company, 2017. |
    "Christy Ottaviano Books." | Summary: In this version of Shakespeare's famous
    love story set in present-day Paris, Romeo and Juliet, heirs to the rival fashion houses
    of Montague and Capulet, share a secret relationship until a mysterious American
    befriends the young lovers.
Identifiers: LCCN 2016035862 (print) | LCCN 2017011050 (ebook) |
    ISBN 978-1-62779-250-9 (hardcover) | ISBN 978-1-250-10948-4 (ebook)
Subjects: | CYAC: Love—Fiction. | Paris (France) —Fiction.
Classification: LCC PZ7.1.S33658 Ro 2017 (print) | LCC PZ7.1.S33658 (ebook) |
    DDC [Fic]—dc23
LC record available at https://lccn.loc.gov/2016035862

Our books may be purchased in bulk for promotional, educational, or business use.
Please contact your local bookseller or the Macmillan Corporate and Premium Sales
Department at (800) 221-7945 ext. 5442 or by e-mail at MacmillanSpecialMarkets@
macmillan.com.

First Edition—2017
Printed in the United States of America by LSC Communications, Harrisonburg,
Virginia
10 9 8 7 6 5 4 3 2 1

TO MOM, FOR TAKING ME OUT OF NURSERY SCHOOL
ONE AFTERNOON TO SEE MY VERY FIRST PLAY,
ROMEO AND JULIET, AND FOR EVERYTHING ELSE.
—L. S.

TO THE COMEDIES AND THE TRAGEDIES AND
THE ONES WHO ARE THE BEST OF BOTH,
BUT MOST OF ALL TO MY LOVE, SJS.
—I-M. P.

PROLOGUE

DON'T SKIP THIS PART.

C'est important. (That's French for exactly what you think.)

In this world, some of us love and some of us write about it.

And the best loves to write about, in my not-inexperienced opinion, are the doomed ones.

Two feuding families: the Montagues and Capulets. Two teens in love: Romeo and Juliet. Yes, one a Montague, one a Capulet. Call them star-crossed if you want. Sounds like just the kind of pretty thing you want to read in your horoscope, but, alas, it's just poet-speak for *doomed.*

So doomed, in fact, you have to wonder if the young beauties can even survive to the end.

We're in Paris, that picture-perfect paradise of everlasting passion. But if you think the City of Love is only for couples who wear their hearts on their sleeves for the world to see, *vous pensez mal*. Paris and its hidden spots are made for forbidden pairs rendezvousing in secret rooms for stolen moments.

And that's exactly what Romeo and Juliet are wont to do. Yes, two rich kids who can buy anything, stealing moments.

Why should two such pretty youths have so much trouble but for a kiss? Oh, for more than that, yes, but still . . . such sneaking shouldn't be necessary. But it goes deep between two families, fueled by hate that's brewed for years.

Two families of fashion, Paris's oldest profession (after the really old one, anyway).

Designs and shipments stolen, reputations dirtied, heirs dethroned, demolished. Even rumors of murder most foul.

And, perhaps, the secrets kept by two old companies dressing up struggles they're hiding from everyone. Both putting on an act, both thinking the other is stronger. They could be in the same support group, but a habit of mutual hatred never goes out of style.

Without a care for old grudges, Romeo Montague and Juliet Capulet are in love.

Star-crossed? Maybe. Doomed? Well, I told you I like that word.

On the verge of meeting a fateful third party even the stars never imagined?

Read on.

CHAPTER 1

JULIET

JULIET RACED ALONG the right bank of the Seine. Tourists walked in slow-moving romantic pairs, shoulders and hips together, each set like a locked gateway blocking her path.

"Excuse me, *excusez-moi, s'il vous plait . . . pardonnez-moi. . . .*"

She slipped between the couples, glad she'd worn fairy-light flats that made her steps soft and fast. Anything heavier, louder, and someone would have stopped to ask her where she'd found that shoulder-skimming button-down (old shirt of her brother's), or who made the black-and-brown leather belt softened with age that cinched her waist (really two old belts she'd found at flea markets and twisted together; her way of wearing them suggested a designer who'd worked hard to engineer them that way).

Every second she lost now was a second lost with him, and those seconds were already so fleeting and infrequent her heart could barely stand it.

She turned onto the Pont des Arts, the metal footbridge that spanned the Seine. She started reading names.

Chantal et Louis

José y Sabrina

Alex and Elizabeth

Jean et Pierre

Guillaume et Penelope

The locks never stopped, and they were all wrong.

Juliet tried not to interrupt moments between lovers as she ducked between them, hoping for a closer look at the locks fastened to the Love-Lock Bridge.

To any tourist on the Seine, Juliet was just another lovelorn girl mooning over each padlocked promise, hoping that one day she'd have someone to vow forever with. After all, there was something far more romantic about this bridge of promises than even the top of the Eiffel Tower at dusk. Lovers would come here with their padlocks or buy a lock from the vendors lining the bridge. They'd write their names and a note on the lock—*Eternité* was a popular phrase—and secure it to the bridge's side. Then, together, they'd hurl the key to the lock into the river, a promise to be fused together ever after.

Most of these pairs knew nothing of what real love was. Juliet was probably being unfair, but to her, the obstacles she and her love faced made their bond more real. So many of these couples, she thought, were tourists in Paris and mere visitors on the course of true love. The real thing never did run smooth.

Yes, the tourists may have seen a forlorn girl, longing for love. But the truth was, she wasn't studying the locks, wishing for one of her own, but was searching for the one that was hers, the one that would lead her to the one who had put it there. *Her* one.

She sidestepped a pair of lovers locked in an embrace, oblivious to everyone, and she felt a tremor of jealousy. She and her love should have been one of those couples, lost in each other, and instead here she was, wasting valuable time trying to find the message that would lead her to him. She reminded herself again that the difficulties she and her lover endured to see each other just meant their love was that much stronger.

Juliet paced the side of the bridge facing Notre-Dame Cathedral. The church was another symbol for them. If their love couldn't be consecrated on earth, it was surely a gift from the heavens.

The locks here were packed tight, and blurred together whenever she stared too long. How would she find theirs?

She took a deep breath, imagining his face, his smile when she arrived. There, in the soft breeze, a red ribbon edged with gold piping fluttered. "Heartstring," they called it. "It's what ties us," he'd said.

Juliet got down onto her knees and took the lock in her hands as tenderly as if it had been his face. Romeo had been here to clasp the lock to the bridge, and, somehow, she could feel him there, that past version of him. She wondered if he'd been able to sense her, this future version of her, finding the lock.

The lock was small but the words written in red marker were clear: *Hotel Lemieux, room 328.*

Juliet's heart pounded so hard she had to run to give it the room it needed in her chest. She hailed a cab as quickly as she could and slipped inside.

"Hotel Lemieux, *s'il vous plait,*" she said.

"Pardon?"

The cab driver turned in his seat and looked at her. Juliet trembled with nerves and bent her head, letting her dark hair fall in waves over her cheeks. The less he saw of her, the better. She wasn't famous, per se, but she was a public figure.

Juliet murmured the address. Most people with money to spend on cabs weren't headed to the Hotel Lemieux. Its name translated to "the best," but in truth the place was a mere step above a youth hostel. The décor and supposed amenities—just a lounge off the lobby housing dusty imitation Louis XIV furniture and a sputtering vending machine—were at least twice Juliet's age. Most of the clientele were young, like Juliet, but not native Parisians. The youthful travelers mostly had nothing but over-stuffed backpacks and dreams of seeing the world.

Juliet loved it there. It may have been close to her and Romeo's homes, but it was so far removed from their worlds that it seemed like anything could happen there. She loved it for the same reasons she loved digging up finds at flea markets and rummage sales: She liked things that belonged to the real world, and not the one her family had created.

Getting there, however, wasn't always easy. Her taxi plodded through Paris traffic, giving her time to think about the latest message that had arrived from Romeo. It was from an account they shared—where they saved emails as drafts for the other to see. Both families had private security details that scanned all incoming and outgoing email. With the shared account, Romeo and Juliet skirted the threat of discovery. The message, without subject, contained just three letters: *A.V.O.* It was her clue to find their lock on the bridge.

Amor Vincit Omnia. Love Conquers All.

It was a phrase she'd discovered while doing research for her father, of all things. It had been three years since she'd found it. Even then, at thirteen, she was already a vaunted figure at the House of Capulet thanks to her innate sense of style. Family legend said that even as a baby, she'd cry if outfitted in the usual princess-pink baby clothes, and looked her most comfortable in more sophisticated ensembles. (She'd had a black velvet party dress as a toddler that was copied a million times over after a photo of her wearing it accompanied a profile of the Capulets that appeared in *Paris Match*.) Juliet just *knew*. Not only with fashion, but with the business. She knew when a brand name would catch such fire it would become part of everyday vernacular, or when a model's unique look would start a major trend.

And at thirteen, she'd been tasked to find a name for a new clothing line for young women approaching adulthood, and "A.V.O." had been her answer. What woman didn't want to believe that true love was the be-all-end-all force to vanquish any threat to happiness?

When she'd found the phrase, she believed it as a young teen who knew nothing of real love. Now, she felt it to her core.

His email had arrived yesterday. Juliet's comings and goings were so tightly monitored that she'd had to wait for an opportunity to sneak across the city, and on Saturdays the house teemed with too much help to slip away. Today, though, her mother had succeeded in dragging her father to church, certainly to be followed by a lavish lunch and shopping excursion. Juliet had left a note that she'd needed to go to the library, for school, and to get some air.

Romeo, well, sometimes he felt like her air.

So, what if he wasn't there anymore? If she arrived at Hotel Lemieux to find he'd gone? She checked her secret email account constantly, obsessively, but that didn't mean she could exit her life at a moment's notice to meet him. He understood and knew the pressures, but thanks to his past, his own family *expected* him to disappear sometimes. He was a young man—a wealthy, dashing one—and sowing his wild oats, as it were, was practically a birthright. It was a birthright he'd easily given up for Juliet, but no one knew that. Not even Juliet. Not yet.

The taxi turned onto the narrow street where the hotel was. A delivery truck blocked the road as workers at a grocer's shop unloaded boxes of produce. Impatience rattled her body.

"This is good," she told the cab driver. "I'll get out now." The hotel was only a few blocks away. She thrust some euros into his palm and leaped out of the cab, running to the hotel and up the stairs as fast as she could until she reached room 328. She knocked.

Please be here. . . . Please be here. . . .

The door clicked open almost instantly. He smiled down at her and her breath stopped. She'd been around the most coveted male models and movie stars in the world, but he was the only one who could render her breathless. Just him.

"I've missed you," Romeo said. He curled his fingers beneath her belt and pulled her to him.

Juliet wrapped her arms around his neck, and as their lips met, the world around them retracted until they were all that was left.

"I thought I'd be too late," Juliet murmured later. Her hair spilled over Romeo's arm. She lay in the crook of his elbow, memorizing the way his bare skin felt beneath her cheek. Tracing the contours of his chest with her fingertips, she felt so at peace at that moment that it could have been seconds or years from the time he'd greeted her at the door. The covers—clean sheets but worn thin after years of service—lay in a tangled heap at their feet. The sheer drapes on the window floated over them as a light breeze pushed through the cracked window. Juliet, who normally slept beneath a goose-down duvet because she was so cold at night, was warm to the touch. His touch.

"You could never be too late. How do you not know by now that I'd wait a lifetime if I had to?"

"Or until your father called. *Romeo, it's an emergency. . . .*" She imitated the voice of Jean Montague, which she'd heard at many fashion industry fetes.

"Juliet . . ."

He scolded her, but gently. From the very beginning, they'd promised each other they wouldn't mar their rare moments together with petulance, frustration, or jealousy. True love came at a price, or theirs did, and they'd vowed to pay it without complaint. But Juliet sometimes had trouble.

"That was mean. I'm sorry," she said, pressing her lips to his chest.

"And it's not just *my* father," Romeo added.

"You're right," Juliet agreed, thinking of how often she was summoned to Capulet duties, even if some of the duties were just to be the pretty apple of her father's eye. She felt so good when she was with Romeo, felt such a sense of possibility, that it almost killed her that who they were mattered so much. Together, they should have been unstoppable, not living in secret.

In a single motion, she quickly rolled over and straddled him. She grinned down at him, a mussed tress of her hair falling against his nose. "Let's do it."

Romeo laughed. "Um, I think we just did. Give me a minute."

Juliet bounced on him, swatting his upper arm playfully. "Not that *it*. The real *it*. We leave. Run away. We'll find somewhere no one's ever been. We'd be following our stars."

Romeo's eyes crinkled with his smile. "So, the uncharted island? Romantic. And how are we going to find it?"

"We'll steal one of our fathers' yachts, of course. You know how to sail."

"And they wouldn't geo-track us instantly?"

"Fine, we'll buy a yacht with unmarked bills. Then we'll get out to sea and sail away until we find the spot. The perfect spot . . ."

"The perfect spot *if* we don't get lost at sea and starve to death."

"We'll be like Adam and Eve, living in beautiful innocence."

"We're not exactly innocent," Romeo quipped, aiming for a kiss.

Juliet pulled away, still smiling. "Don't shoot me down. I'm serious."

"I just don't see how we'd survive. No electricity, no shelter, no soap . . . and we haven't exactly been raised with amazing survival skills." Romeo arched an eyebrow at her.

She loved the crackle behind his eyes but hated that its purpose now was to reject her idea. Juliet sighed and rolled off Romeo onto the mattress next to him. "Fine. We don't need an island. We'll go to America. A small town, where no one would know us or ever think to look. We'll change our names, find a tiny apartment. . . ."

"And pay rent with money we won't have, because we'll be cut off from our fortunes."

"With money we'll grab in cash and bring with us so we'll have it after we're cut off. . . ."

"And when it runs out?"

"I'll design clothes, you'll market them."

"Yes, teen runaways always launch amazing start-ups."

"Well, it doesn't have to be clothes. I'd wait tables or work a cash register somewhere if it meant being with you. . . ." Juliet trailed off. She scanned his face, fighting a tear. "You don't love me at all."

Every hint of play and daydream left Romeo's face. Juliet trembled at the intensity beneath his icy-blue eyes as he rolled to face her. "I don't love you?" he echoed fiercely. "I love you so much it eats me alive. Every moment of every day, I think about you and ache for you. And then we're together and I'm full and empty and sick because I know how awful it's going to be to let you go."

Juliet caressed his cheek. "Then don't. Don't let me go." She, too, knew the sick feeling, and was experiencing it now as she thought about their time together ending. "Let's run away."

Romeo smiled sadly and laced his fingers with hers. He squeezed her hand once, then twice, then three times, and in those small squeezes, she felt his love more acutely than even when they kissed, or when he told her in no uncertain terms. Touch was better than words. "There's no *away*," he whispered. "We're not people who can disappear. We're not children whose families wouldn't look for us. We're not people who can't be found. And if they learn we're together . . ."

"Let them," Juliet said. "What can they do once we're gone?" She tried to sound defiant and strong, but she knew.

"They'll ruin us."

Their families were powerful, with resources others could

only dream of. If they wanted to, it would be easy for them to keep Romeo and Juliet apart forever. It would be easy to banish them to lives that were impoverished in ways beyond the financial. They could be separated, lost to each other and rendered almost identity-less. The families had the means to do so.

"Above all else, loyalty." Juliet shuddered as she spoke her father's mantra. Her brother had nearly been cast out of the family. Henri had been at his lowest when he sold prints of some Capulet designs to the House of Montague (which had turned them into—insult on injury—a low-priced line for Montague IV, a chain of stores in American malls). He had been near death, crippled by his addictions, but all that had seemed to matter to their father was Henri's betrayal. The family had tossed Henri into a literal dungeon to detox—painfully—and now he was forced to play his part as if he'd never been anything other than the perfect son. Poor Henri's birthright, the inheritance of the House of Capulet, was even threatened. Not that he seemed to care. But what they could do to her was much worse. She looked at Romeo, imagining a life completely devoid of him.

"Don't think on it." Romeo wrapped his arms around her and kissed her like he was breathing life back into her body. Taking her face in his hands, he stared into her eyes, pulling her back into the moment with his gaze. "I won't let that happen. Not to either of us. But you see why we have to stay strong."

"You shouldn't have been born a Montague," Juliet said. "Or I shouldn't have been born a Capulet. What I'd give to just be some Girl Nobody for you to discover and love. . . ."

"You're so wrong," Romeo said, his lips curved in the half smile she loved. "I wouldn't change a thing. The stars crossed to unite us. Our curses are our blessings, too. You don't mess with that kind of gift."

"Patience, then," Juliet said. They'd been through this before; her lines were clear. But every time they were together, she imagined things could go differently.

Romeo kissed her, a kiss that unfolded slowly, opening her lips like petals, then pressing his mouth more urgently to hers. "Time is on our side."

"I hate being patient," Juliet said. "I love you. I want you."

She skimmed her leg over his body and raised herself above him. She kissed him back until her mind stopped working. She wanted him, and she had her wish. For those moments, she wasn't a Capulet; he wasn't a Montague. They were themselves, Romeo and Juliet, and they were one.

CHAPTER 2

ROMEO

HE HATED SAYING no to her. He didn't *want* to say no to her. She lay across his chest, dozing lightly while he twirled a piece of her hair around his finger and studied the way the light hit the chocolatey strands. He wished he wasn't a lousy poet and could say something about how he felt, but words fell short. So, instead, he gazed at her and thought to wake her, to say, *Let's go. Go . . .* wherever she wanted. Because she made him want to.

And these weren't the musings of some uninformed idiot who'd never been with a woman before. He'd been, and been, and been.

She was singular, uncommon, and perfect for him—of this there was no doubt.

He'd probably known from the start, a month and a half ago.

He'd been leaving the studio apartment of an artist he was seeing, a woman in her twenties who liked to paint in the nude. Her lithe back was itself a work of art, tattooed in a collage of Art Deco–era women, short-haired in feathered headbands, holding fans, peering out through painted eyes. The effect was mesmerizing. And the artist was a beautiful, slinky creation herself. But he knew he'd grow bored of her gallery eventually. . . .

Still, for two days he'd been ensconced with her, only coming up for a little air and coffee and cigarettes, when he'd been summoned back to his life by his father, who knew about and allowed Romeo's "hobbies." He'd kissed the artist good-bye and dashed out onto the street below her apartment in Montmartre. There'd been a street fair, which meant slow, strolling shoppers, and he was making his way through a cluster of women browsing a selection of old scarves when he saw Juliet.

He knew who she was, of course. Before he could even form memories, he'd no doubt been shown photos of her, likely labeled "Capulet: Mortal Enemy." But now, with the sunlight just hitting his eyes again (the artist kept heavy curtains drawn always), he blinked, not believing one of the heirs to his rival would be rummaging through secondhand goods.

They'd been going to the same school since Juliet had transferred there earlier in the year. She was no doubt attractive, even captivating, but he had always imagined her to be a princess and knew her to be a Capulet, so he'd never let himself pay her too much attention.

That day in Montmartre, an idea formed in Romeo's mind. Not an idea so much as a big *Why not?* It would be a little fun to see if he could render Juliet Capulet breathless. He wouldn't let it go too far, of course.

She was carrying two heavy-looking tote bags, one on each shoulder. Corners of old hardcovers poked out the tops. She looked unfazed by the weight as she picked up pieces of costume jewelry from a table and smiled and chatted with the old man on a stool behind the booth.

Romeo sauntered through the crowd toward her, his confidence in his game—and the fact that he had the added power of being forbidden fruit—making him feel like this was going to be too easy.

He came up next to her, and she turned and glanced at him. Her eyes were dark brown and flecked with gold. Intelligent eyes that locked with his for a split second before she turned back to looking at the merchandise.

Sucker-punched was the only word to describe what he felt then. His tongue went still in his mouth, his hands shook, and his chest hurt. He found himself scanning the same pieces of jewelry, their shoulders almost touching. And even though he'd never had problems coming up with things to say to a woman before, he'd only been able to stand next to her, listening with a dumb grin as she made sly jokes, to the shopkeep's delight, about whether the old man sourced the jewelry from former paramours.

Finally, she selected some jade earrings and paid, then turned on her beat-up riding boots and struck his shoulder with one of the bags.

It jolted Romeo into the moment and he made a quick decision to act as if he didn't know who she was. "Ouch." He rubbed his shoulder in an overdramatic way. "Maybe you need help with your bags?"

She raised her left brow at him, and he knew that she knew who he was, too. But she didn't admit that. She grasped the game instantly. Juliet just said, her lip curling up on one side with amusement, "That's cute, but I bought the things. I think I can carry them." Her dark eyes twinkled as she spoke, but what he noticed were her hands—slim with long, tapered fingers, yet strong and capable, like she used them to make things.

"Stubborn," he teased. "I don't know about that."

"Keep an open mind. Being stubborn is important to me," she parried back, moving into the crowd. He fell into step next to her as she visited the next few stalls, asking questions about this scarf or that brooch as she held them up, seeming to have plans for each one.

"You like old things?" he said.

"Some old, some new." She smiled. "But mostly things that not everyone has, or not everyone knows they want."

Every word she spoke was confident but not condescending. He was bewitched by her easy take on things, and by how someone who could have been a princess seemed to prefer being just a member of the public, albeit a gimlet-eyed observer instead of a blind follower. (Romeo had romanced his fair share of the public who hoped to be made princesses through his affections, and now he was trying to woo the one person who seemed uninterested in any such thing.)

The stars had aligned for them that day, and neither of them had thought for a second what a danger it would be to be seen together. It was March and the first nice day after a cold, gray winter, and everyone in Paris was unconcerned with anyone but themselves and their own sunlit comfort. They talked and walked until the shopkeepers began to put away their wares and fold up their tables.

Romeo remembered, only then, that he had to get back to his father, and the dangerous way he'd been consorting with—hell, *falling* for—the enemy hit him in the gut. "You know, we shouldn't be doing this," he said as the slanting afternoon sun seemed to draw away from them, leaving them standing in shadows.

"Doing what? Talking?" Juliet said, and peered at him with a little smile. "We don't have to talk." She still had the bags of books on her shoulders. He'd made several more offers and she'd refused his help, in the most guileless way imaginable.

She didn't need him, at all, but he could tell she liked him. Maybe even liked him the way he did her.

And then she'd kissed him on the cheek and said, "You're very sweet." *Sweet,* a word no one ever called him. "We'll see each other again."

She'd left him in suspense for a week—he'd looked for her in the halls of their school but she seemed to have vanished. Then he'd found a note from her tucked, somehow, in his bag. *Samedi,*

12:30 p.m. and the name of a teahouse in Petite Asie, where no one ever went.

They'd met and talked and talked about how they could talk more—she'd come up with the idea of the secret email account and sending nothing, just writing each other drafts. And it had been her idea to go somewhere more private, and she'd chosen the Hotel Lemieux. "Are you sure?" he'd said as she led him by the hand up the stairs. He'd almost been trembling when she closed the door. But then, in the privacy they'd afforded themselves, he'd needed to kiss her.

That first kiss was an affirmation of all they'd both suspected: There was nothing ordinary about them.

"We can wait," he'd said.

"You don't wait when it might be your only chance," she'd told him, as sure about that as she was about everything.

He just wished, now, that he could reward her certainty without certain destruction.

CHAPTER 3

JULIET

AN HOUR LATER, Juliet beamed as she and Romeo skimmed down the last flight of steps and into the lobby. Their hands locked together felt as decadent and effervescent as the bubbles surging in a glass of Dom Pérignon White Gold Jeroboam. The buzz was even more delicious.

"If I could put the feeling of holding your hand in broad daylight in capsule form, we'd make a fortune," Juliet said as they stepped out onto the street, full of hustling backpackers and hardscrabble immigrants. Here, they were completely invisible. No one in this neighborhood cared about Capulets and Montagues. It was why she'd chosen it, last month, hoping that it could become their place. It had, even if this was only the third time they'd gotten to be together there.

"That is extremely lovely," Romeo said, pulling Juliet into him. She leaned her head on his shoulder as they strolled into Paris's Chinatown, where the smells of dim sum and Peking duck spiced the air.

"Lovely but also lucrative," Juliet said. "Are you sure you don't want to trust my visions and set sail?" She lightened her tone so he'd know she was joking, but she did—either through naive optimism or shrewd awareness of how everyone in the world desired a romance like theirs—believe they'd make it, even as she knew Romeo was right about all the flaws in her plans.

They were on their way to their favorite restaurant, a ramshackle teahouse where neither the owners nor the rest of the clientele spoke any French, but that had the most delicious oolong tea Romeo and Juliet had ever tasted. Or, at least, they thought it did, since this was their place. They ducked inside and found their favorite seats, beneath a low-falling eave at a table that might have felt claustrophobic to anyone else but them. Once there, they turned their phones back on, as they did after each meeting.

They'd just had their first warming sips of oolong when the noise from the street outside rose several decibels. Monsieur Y, the teahouse owner, stood at the door, speaking to a man with a large camera hanging from his neck.

"I'm sorry to not have a permit, but we can give you cash to shoot here," the photographer was telling Monsieur Y. "Huge campaign, so you'll be paid well. The only thing is, we need you to decide now."

Romeo looked across the table at Juliet, concern etched on his face. "This doesn't sound good," he said. "We can't be here if photographers come in." He opened his wallet and put more than the needed amount of euros on the table.

"Should we go out the back?" Juliet said, her heart racing. Much as she could talk the talk of a defiant woman in love, she knew what being photographed together would do to them.

Juliet's phone dinged. The screen read, *Gabrielle nearby!* A little dot on a map appeared, and Gabrielle, it turned out, was very nearby. Just-outside-the-door nearby.

"Oh my God," Juliet whispered.

Gabrielle's distinctive purr oozed through the door.

"Juliet Capulet . . . are you in there? *Why* are you in there?"

Monsieur Y was holding his ground at the door as he negotiated with the photographer, and Romeo and Juliet were well hidden at their table, but still, Gabrielle's voice was a reality check in the worst way.

"How does she know?" Romeo asked.

"We linked our phones so we could find one another when we went shopping last week," Juliet said. "I just didn't turn off the app."

How could she have forgotten? Gabrielle, one of the top models in Paris—nay, Europe—had gone on and on last week when they were out about how she would be doing a shoot in Petite Asie and how she'd have to be extra careful not to pick up any germs from the backpackers. Juliet had felt so smug asking all kinds of questions about the neighborhood that she'd known the answers to. She'd let Gabrielle go on and on about how different it was from their world, and had feigned curiosity, as if she'd never been there.

Though she sometimes wished she could tell Gabrielle everything, Juliet had grown up so sheltered and protected that it was now her way to be wary of even people she called friends. It was part of what made being with Romeo feel so good: She finally felt like she was purely herself with someone, and that she could allow him to really know her.

"Out the back," Juliet said, imagining the way Gabrielle—and an army of fashion magazine people—would revel in this gossip. Heads would roll, just to find other heads to tell everything to.

Juliet and Romeo cut through the small kitchen area, ignoring the shocked faces of the teahouse staff. The alley behind the restaurant was blocked off on one side by the high walls of an apartment building. The open end led to the street, where the entire apparatus of Gabrielle's photo shoot was present. Workers were erecting scaffolding and lights; stylists were rolling racks of clothing along the uneven pavement. This was no small affair, and Romeo and Juliet would not have an easy time emerging from the alleyway undetected.

Juliet's phone buzzed. Gabrielle was calling her. She pressed the button to make it go to voice mail and then shut the phone down.

They were pressed to the back wall of the teahouse, next to a

Dumpster that smelled of rotting discarded food from the dim sum restaurant next door.

Juliet peeked around the corner. Gabrielle was pacing, huffing into her cell phone, probably still calling Juliet. An entourage followed her every step. Steps taken on six-inch heels, each sprouting a plume of peacock feathers that glowed electric blue against her dark-chocolate skin. Gabrielle wore a string bikini made of glittering crystals, red hair extensions blazed out of her head, and her eyes were painted in thick stripes of pink and blue. She was on fire with agitation.

"Why isn't she picking up? My phone said she's right here. Someone get me a cell-phone nerd to figure this out for me."

Gabrielle glanced witheringly at a timid-looking assistant. "Are you sure you didn't see Juliet in there? Dark hair, innocent little face? Like she needs to lose her virginity, stat?"

Despite herself, Juliet stifled a laugh at the fallacy of the comment. Romeo squeezed her hand tight.

Of course Gabrielle couldn't let it rest. This was a part of town neither of them would be in, save for a major fashion magazine shoot or a very secret tryst. Juliet couldn't exactly walk out and say, *"Quelle coincidence!"* like they'd just run into each other at Printemps department store.

Romeo and Juliet were trapped like the rats that haunted this very alley. People might see them, and if those people were Gabrielle and an entire fashion-knowledgeable camera crew, well, they could kiss their secret good-bye. The idea that the very photogenic heirs to the two biggest archrivals of the Paris fashion world were here together, with no discernible reason for being in this part of town other than what they'd just been doing—well, it was the kind of scandal that would be everywhere.

A woman with black glasses and a clipboard approached Gabrielle. "We have to start. . . ."

Gabrielle's response echoed down the alley. "Look, I'm not going to be able to focus on this shoot unless I know why my phone was saying Juliet Capulet was here, and now it's not. That isn't black magic. This is technology! She was here and I want to know why. It will drive me crazy, and crazy doesn't look good on camera."

Juliet shuddered. Her friend was nothing if not determined.

"*Merde, merde, merde,*" Romeo muttered.

Next to the dim sum restaurant, an old man emerged from an open back door, tossing a trash bag into the Dumpster. Music and smoke poured out into the alley.

"Let's go in there—at least it's off the street," Juliet said, and they slid past the man and into a bar. It was small and narrow and utterly nondescript, perhaps why they'd never noticed it before. But it was still too bright inside and too close to the commotion outside. Through a graying window, the scurrying of various photo-shoot personnel was obvious. If Gabrielle was as resolute as she sounded, and if she got the rest of the shoot as riled up as she was about Juliet Capulet slumming it, they would be found within seconds.

At this time of day, there was no crowd to hide in. The only other person in the bar was a man in a vintage motorcycle jacket and black skinny jeans. He hovered over the jukebox, and Juliet couldn't tell if he was poring over the song list or getting ready to punch the machine.

"I can't believe this," Romeo said, with so much horror that Juliet's heart dropped. She knew she'd gotten under his skin talking about running away, but now he seemed almost angry. He clutched his forehead with his hand, pushing his longish hair from his eyes.

"I'm sorry—" Juliet started.

Romeo turned to her and grasped her shoulders. "I'm not mad at you. Never you," he said. "I'm just angry that this is so hard." He looked around. "What if we just hang out?"

"Did you not hear Gabrielle? She's going to turn the neighborhood upside down until she finds me."

"The tall Black girl, with the hair?" the guy at the jukebox asked them. "She was in here with crazy eyes, looking for a Juliet." He had an American accent. "That you?"

Juliet nodded.

"Yeah, don't doubt that she'll be back. I can get you out of here, though," he said.

"What? Why?" Romeo asked. His voice was edged with malice. He stepped forward to place himself between Juliet and the stranger.

"I don't know. Sounds fun. Nothing going on here, clearly."

His eyes glinted as he offered them a half smile. There was an assured carelessness to him that bothered Juliet, though not in an entirely bad way. He was about their age but lighter than them somehow. Unworried. It was a trait that came off a lot of Americans, an amused joie de vivre that eluded French natives.

Out the window, the spikes of Gabrielle's hair extensions crossed Juliet's line of vision.

"Which way?" Juliet said, coming to stand next to Romeo. She took his hand and squeezed, hoping to convey to him that she thought they should take the stranger up on his offer.

"I'm just going to check in here once more," she could hear Gabrielle saying. "I have to know if she's here."

Romeo's shoulders were tense, but he remained immobile despite the threat outside.

The American guy, who was still grinning at them like they were playing a game, looked from Romeo to Juliet with an expression that said, *This is your only option.* He started for the back of the bar. "Bike's this way."

He was so at ease and casual about the escape that Juliet wanted to shake him. After she shook Romeo, of course. She pulled her boyfriend toward the back of the bar and slid through the door just as Gabrielle's voice rang through the empty space, seeming to send dust motes flying with her volume.

"Juliet!" she yelled.

Juliet wondered if she'd been seen. She'd deal with it later. She, Romeo, and the stranger were back outside. And there, on the side of the Dumpster where they hadn't been hiding, was a motorcycle. The stranger was already straddling the saddle, his arm outstretched with a helmet for her. His helmet.

"Tuck your hair under here, it'll help disguise you," he said to her. His fingers brushed hers, and they were rougher than Romeo's, like he'd been working on his bike just before finding them. "Then get on behind me." He smiled again, one corner of his mouth turned up higher than the other. His eyes were espresso-colored, with a golden twinkle in the corners. Gabrielle would have lapped him up, as she liked to say. Juliet suddenly understood the expression.

Looking at Romeo, he pointed to the sidecar. "You'll ride there. Keep your head down."

Juliet strapped on the helmet, smelling what had to be the stranger's sweat on the padding lining the inside. It wasn't unpleasant.

"Come on, already," the stranger said, locking his dark eyes on Juliet's. She shuddered, but not from fear.

"I don't like this," Romeo said, sinking down into the sidecar like it was a cold, uncomfortable bath. But still, he pulled his hood up over his light hair and hunched his shoulders.

"We don't have a choice," Juliet said. She tentatively reached her arms around the stranger's taut waist. If her mother had had any idea that an hour ago she'd been in bed with Romeo and now she was entwined on a motorcycle with this gorgeous American, well, Hélène Capulet would die on the spot. But not without first shooting Juliet an icy look of disdain. Her mother hadn't fought her way from the chaos of a well-off but dysfunctional family into a wealthy, if staid, life just so her daughter could make the kind of mistakes that made a person wonder if vice was hereditary. Henri had already proven a challenge.

Taking her hands, the stranger made her grip him tighter. "Like this, unless you want to fall into the street."

"What's your name?" Juliet shouted over the noise of the bike starting up. She felt the need to talk casually, so she wouldn't dwell on how tightly she was holding on to this person. The muscles along his sides clenched as he revved the bike a few times.

"Jim," he said. "I'm Jim."

He kicked the bike up to speed and maneuvered past the fashion-shoot commotion on the street. Juliet kept her eyes closed, as if that would disguise her.

But no one even looked, since Gabrielle had everyone in a tizzy looking inside the bar. Jim leaned into the turn around the corner, and he, Romeo, and Juliet sped away, undetected.

WHENEVER TWO YOUNG lovers are forced to speed away from witnesses on the back of a stranger's motorbike, one must stop to ask: *Pourquoi?*

They're two rich, beautiful teens with everything. Shouldn't their families be thrilled they're together? They're a perfect match, an instant power couple—the tabloids would brand them Juleo, or Roliet!

Sadly, that's not at all the case, thanks to an ancient grudge. No one is quite sure exactly how it started, but it goes back to the days when the families lived in castles, and back when the French stopped wearing armor and started donning gowns and robes, cinching waists and peacocking about, fully plumed.

Yes, both the ancient families, Capulet and Montague, one day long ago decided to make fashion their business. (Other families, too, but they were the best at it, or at least the most well-known.)

Then someone stepped on someone's bustle and all hell broke loose. It might sound frivolous—an ancient feud over fashion?—but they take it very seriously. So seriously that the grudge has endured through the centuries—property destroyed, lives ruined . . . some lives lost (or taken). That neither family is sure why the grudge began is no matter, because keeping it alive is a matter of principle at this point.

So, yes, the rich, beautiful teens seem to have everything, but ages of cultivated hate and pride means they will always be denied what they want most: each other.

CHAPTER 4

ROMEO

WHAT IDIOT GOT in the sidecar of a motorcycle piloted by a son-of-a-bitch American?

What idiot did that, not knowing where they were going?

What idiot let his beautiful girlfriend clutch the son-of-a-bitch American like they were the couple, while he, the idiot, rode in the sidecar?

He didn't like this.

No, Romeo didn't like this at all, that he and Juliet had placed their lives in the hands of some buffed-out American with an action-hero complex.

And he really didn't like that Juliet was pressed up against the guy, spooning her body into his with her arms tight around his waist. Meanwhile, Romeo was scrunched with his knees practically touching his chin, thanks to the case of beer on which he had to rest his feet.

"Where you wanna go?" Jim shouted over the noise of the bike when they reached a red light.

"Here's good," Romeo said. He and Juliet would get off the bike and split up. No parting kiss for them, but they'd be safe. Too bad he was so low to the ground Jim couldn't even hear him.

Juliet, though—Jim could hear her. How could he not? She could almost lick the guy's earlobe. "Where would you go if you didn't want to be seen?" she asked.

The melodic lilt to her voice almost killed Romeo, it was so pretty. Jim must have liked it, too, because he grinned and nodded, probably imagining where he'd take Juliet if they could ditch Romeo. Jerk. When the light changed, he swerved to the left and kicked up his speed.

Romeo had lived his whole life in Paris, as had generations of Montagues before him. He prided himself on knowing every intimate crevice of the city. He was a connoisseur of forbidden hideaways, places to take a lover where they'd never be seen or suspected.

That was all before Juliet, though. His pursuit of conquests had ceased when he met her. The change had almost killed his cousin and best friend, Benoit, who'd been particularly invested in hearing more about the Art Deco–tattooed woman. All the women, really. Once upon a time, Romeo and Benny would spend hours talking in detail about Romeo's activities. Romeo would pull out the onyx lockbox given to him by his grandfather when he was only six. He'd told him it was a *"coffre-fort de Rêves,"* a dream safe, a place where he could store notes about his wildest hopes and fantasies.

Romeo used it for storing the souvenirs of hopes and fantasies that had come to pass. Inside were matchbooks from every low-rent gem in which he'd shared *moments amoureuses* with the finest women in Paris. He had been with wide-eyed girls his own age who dreamed of being together forever and well-preserved older damsels who'd left him panting for more. Romeo could pluck a matchbook from the box at random and call up sordid details to make Benny's jaw drop.

But the night after he'd met Juliet . . . That night, without a second thought, he'd padded down to the living room to start a fire and emptied the box's contents into the flames. He remembered how satisfying it had been to hear the pops and cracks of the matchbooks as they caught fire. He'd gladly tossed out his past, in anticipation of a future with her.

Benny had thrown a fit when he learned the matches were gone. He'd been furious when Romeo had refused to speak again of the old dalliances.

"Bro, those stories are my religion!" he'd wailed. "You're really going to take away a man's religion?"

Romeo wasn't sure Benny would understand even if he could explain, but of course he couldn't. True love was as simple and complex a reason as could exist. Over the last month, Benny had floated a million different theories as to why Romeo had changed, but none of them came close.

Much as Romeo liked to think he knew every last bit of Paris, he had no idea where they were right now. Jim had taken the bike past the hills and odd pastel houses of La Butte-aux-Cailles. Now the ill-maintained streets skirted buildings with chipped masonry and balconies that leaned dangerously off their moorings. The streets were vacant—no outdoor cafés, no shops, no kids playing outside. This wasn't hidden Paris, this was *dying* Paris.

Now that the threat of discovery was gone, a new kind of threat set off red flags in Romeo's head. Who was this American? He could be angling to rob them—or worse. Romeo had to plan his next move very carefully.

Jim turned the motorcycle onto the overgrown lawn of an old, crumbling stone church. He pulled around back, where ancient headstones sprouted from the ground at odd angles like stone weeds. Jim cut the bike's engine but remained still. Juliet's hands dropped to her sides as she pulled her body away from his.

Jim turned in his seat, looking at Romeo but speaking to Juliet. Romeo's body tensed as he prepared himself to spring from the sidecar. What he'd do next, he wasn't exactly sure.

"Frisk me," Jim said to Juliet.

"What?" she asked.

"Your boyfriend's looking at me like he wants to jump up and go all Napoléon on my ass," Jim said. "You've already had your hands on me. So frisk me and let him know I don't have a weapon."

Juliet looked at Romeo, a question in her eyes. Romeo really didn't want her to touch more of the guy than she already had, but he knew it would answer his questions. He nodded his consent, and Juliet patted her hands over Jim's leather jacket, starting at the top and working her way to his waist.

"There is nothing," she said.

"Aw, come on," Jim said. "That's just insulting."

Juliet blushed.

"Enough," Romeo said, then told Jim, "Don't move."

Romeo leaped as nimbly as he could out of the sidecar and gestured for Jim to stand up. Romeo was taller, but lean, while Jim had a compact, muscular build. Romeo patted his jacket aggressively, trying to let Jim know he wasn't intimidated. He locked eyes with the American, daring him to make a move.

"Dude, I'm one of the good guys, I swear," Jim said. "You were the ones who needed a getaway car. I should be frisking *you*."

"Don't," Romeo warned.

Jim raised his hands in a *Who, me?* gesture. Romeo took Juliet by the hands to help her off the bike. He let his hands linger at Juliet's hip, as if to show Jim that she belonged to him.

"Where are we?" Juliet asked. She walked in a slow circle around a gravestone, then tilted her head skyward, looking like a misplaced angel.

"Seriously?" Jim replied. "The Ugly American knows more than the natives?"

"I never called you ugly," Juliet noted.

"Oh, well, thank you, then," Jim said, grinning. Romeo didn't like the easy way he made eye contact with Juliet, like they'd known each other for years.

Jim pulled three bottles of beer out of the case in the sidecar and handed one to each of them.

Juliet blushed as she took the bottle. Romeo draped a possessive arm around her shoulders and held out his beer. "Got an opener?"

"Of course," Jim said. He strode to the closest tombstone and used its edge to pry off the bottlecap. He handed the beer back to Romeo, who tried not to show his annoyance at being schooled in bottle opening by the self-assured American.

"As to where we are," Jim started, as he spread his arms wide and walked backward, gesturing to the entire cemetery. "We're nowhere. An abandoned church in an abandoned part of town." He sat down on the grass and leaned against one of the ancient headstones, popping the cap off his bottle, too. "An excellent place for a drink."

Then he took a long swig of his beer, before pointing his bottle at the stones opposite him, a gesture for Romeo and Juliet to sit. Romeo looked down at Juliet. He wondered if she'd be spooked by the whole scene, but she had a giddy glimmer in her eyes instead. She rose on her tiptoes to kiss him.

"Liberté, mon amour," she whispered to him with her sly little grin.

Freedom. Yes. To be sure, even in this quiet graveyard they weren't really free, but at least, for a time, no one would find them. But it was dicey enough that the bars on Romeo's cell phone were spotty. He was almost a phantom here, same as this American.

"Liberté," Romeo replied.

Juliet beamed, then pulled Romeo down to sit on the lawn, across from Jim. Romeo used a headstone to pop the cap off Juliet's beer, giving Jim a look that said, *I can be macho, too.* He sat against a tombstone with his feet planted on the ground and his knees bent, so Juliet could curl into the armchair made by his chest and parted legs. He raised an eyebrow at Jim and lifted his bottle in an unspoken toast. And, he hoped, an unspoken threat to never call Romeo "Napoléon" again. Jim mirrored the gesture and they both drank.

"So, now you must tell us about yourself," Juliet told Jim. "My boyfriend doesn't seem to trust you, and I trust his opinion on everything."

"Wow, good girlfriend," Jim said. "But there's not much to tell. Life's pretty simple."

"Yes, a simple life full of vintage Harleys with sidecars, all in mint condition?" Romeo gestured to the bike.

Now Jim smiled openly. It was the kind of machismo-laden grin that seemed mastered only by Americans. He could probably run fast, too. "You noticed that, huh?"

"My boyfriend has an unquenchable lust for fast, flashy things," Juliet said. "I'm very lucky that extends only to his vehicles."

"I prefer my women beautiful and mesmerizing," Romeo said.

"And I like mine gorgeous and crazy," Jim said. "At least according to my track record."

"Typical guy," Juliet snorted. "Things go wrong and you say the girl is crazy. Maybe the blame's on you? After all, is it not crazy to pick up strangers and hang out in abandoned cemeteries?"

"Point well taken," Jim agreed. "But either way, I think I've learned it's best for me to stay away from women. At least for now. Present company excluded, of course."

"Of course," Juliet said. "Though while I'm fairly sane, I've been quite rude. My name is Beatrix. This handsome backrest is Benedict." She squeezed Romeo's leg, alerting him to pay attention to her lie. He loved her even more for knowing to give fake names. So he pulled her in closer, relishing the gentle rise of her back against his chest as she breathed.

"Pleased to meet you," Jim said. "Even under the circumstances. You know, I'd really like to know what was going on back there. But I'm going to mind my own business."

"That's not very American of you," Romeo said.

"Nah, but you're not an entirely rude French person, so we're even." With his easy grin, he nodded toward his Harley and looked back at Romeo. "You have a bike of your own?"

"A couple," Romeo admitted. "I bought a Wattman for my birthday."

"Voxon?" Jim asked. "The electric? It's supposed to run like a beast."

"A gorgeous beast," Romeo said. "Looks like a scorpion."

"I'd love to take a spin on that sometime," Jim said. "Seriously."

"And I would love to change the subject to anything but motorcycles. Or cars," Juliet groaned. "I could start talking about fashion, but I don't think any of us want that."

Romeo laughed, but not for the reason he knew Jim thought. As heir apparent to the House of Montague, Paris's other oldest and most respected fashion house, Romeo could just as happily carry on an intelligent conversation about trending necklines as he could the best places to trick out a Harley. So Juliet's comment was a ruse. She was playing a role: normal girl. Beatrix. The kind of girl who could just hang out, leaning against him, casually—almost wickedly—throwing the words *my boyfriend* into the conversation. Romeo could tell from her tone that she loved it.

He did, too. Dangerously so. If it kept up, he'd start talking like Juliet about running away. And he had to stay grounded. He knew Juliet hated when he pulled apart her daydreams, but he had to protect the two of them.

Still, couldn't he be grounded a little later? They were, somehow, safe and free. The conversation had been steered at Juliet's request away from motorized vehicles and onto skiing, which all of them loved. Jim swore Colorado was wildly overrated; he said Jackson Hole, Wyoming, was the only legit place to ski in the US. Juliet agreed but expounded on the virtues of Andermatt, Switzerland. Jim was saying Verbier was a superior spot in that country.

"Yeah, if you care about dance clubs more than actual snow," Romeo said.

"Okay, maybe I'll give you that," Jim said.

The guys cracked second beers. Juliet was still nursing her first. Romeo didn't even think of how much time had passed until he glanced up and saw how low the sun had sunk in the sky. The horizon beyond the cemetery was heavy with plump orange clouds. Alarm chilled his veins.

He pulled out his cell phone again, and this time noticed a trail of unanswered calls and messages from his parents and Benoit that he must have overlooked in the excitement.

"*Merde,*" he said.

"What?" Juliet asked, placing her beer bottle in the grass.

"Palais Galliera," he said.

Juliet gasped, then scrambled for her own phone, which she'd never turned back on after shutting it off to avoid Gabrielle's tracking.

Pallais Galliera was Paris's fashion museum, and tonight was the night of an inaugural costume ball, sponsored by *Maintenant,* one of the top fashion magazines in Europe. Representives of both the House of Montague and the House of Capulet were expected to attend, and by this time in the evening, Romeo and Juliet would normally be at home, getting prepared.

Romeo read the text from Benny: *Dude, better have a detailed story and a new matchbook for me. Totally saved your ass telling your parents you were getting some last-minute alterations on a new tux.*

Thank God. He had a little time. "Things okay?"

"Messages from Maman and Lu Hai," Juliet said. "And a million from Gabrielle."

He wished Juliet would lose Gabrielle as a friend. He didn't have to know her in person to know that Gabrielle's thoughts revolved around how to create drama. All you had to do was glance at the tabloids and their stories about the many broken hearts Gabrielle left in her wake, even if Juliet claimed that the other broken hearts were just her friend's efforts to hide the fact that Gabrielle's own heart belonged to Juliet's brother, Henri. Whatever the truth, with suspicions in her mind, Gabrielle would be all over Juliet, pumping her for details about today.

"It'll be fine," Juliet assured him. "I'll make something up. I really don't think she saw us."

Romeo nodded, still doubtful, but confident that Juliet's mental prowess exceeded Gabrielle's. He turned to Jim. "We need to go," he said. "Can you give us a ride?"

"Sure," Jim said, rising and dusting off the sleeves of his jacket. "Where you headed?"

"Will you take me to the Metro at Tolbiac, not far from where we met? And Ju—Beatrix—to Avenue Montaigne."

Juliet laughed out loud. "Oh, yes, have the mysterious American drop me off at my door. No, you take me to Monceau Metro station, please. You know where it is?"

Jim nodded with a grin. Romeo felt a frisson of envy at the way Juliet called him "the mysterious American," but reassured himself that it was nothing.

"So," Jim said, "are we going to hang out again, or was this a one-day stand?"

The question was directed more to Romeo than to Juliet. Romeo smiled. Jim knew not to mess with his girl.

"Give us your number," Romeo said. "We'll call you."

CHAPTER 5

JULIET

"UM, WHEN ARE you going to tell me what you were doing in Petite Asie?"

"I don't know what you're talking about," Juliet said into her phone, putting as much puzzlement in her voice as she could. The Metro was loud around her and she hoped the background noise would help disguise the tremor she knew came into her voice when she lied.

"Oh, really?" Gabrielle said. "So why did you pop up on my phone? 'Juliet nearby!' It doesn't say that if you're not nearby. And why would I almost swear on my gorgeous but cruel mother's grave that I saw that enviable hair of yours disappearing out the back door of a sleazy bar?"

"Maybe you needed to eat something," Juliet teased. "You know how light-headed you get when you're fasting."

"Fasting my ass," Gabrielle said. "I know you were there."

"Yes, I was hanging out in Petite Asie, just drinking during the day and befriending backpackers. That doesn't sound like anything I'd ever do."

"And that is exactly why it's so delicious. So, who was he?"

Juliet's heart caught. Had Gabrielle seen her with Romeo? Or even with Jim? All Gabrielle needed was a morsel to cling to and she'd never let go. Not always in the airheaded way Romeo imagined, either. Gabrielle had spent one day with Henri several years ago and still wasn't over him, even though she pretended otherwise.

"Now you've got me in Petite Asie with a man. Gabrielle, what would I be doing there with a . . . 'he'?" Juliet tried to sound as dumb to the ways of the world as she could, even as her mind replayed parts of her joyous encounter with Romeo.

"You know exactly what you'd be doing! The thing we've all done. Except you. Until now." Gabrielle laughed wickedly into the receiver. "Just tell me who the lucky recipient of your pristine flower was. You know you want to give me details."

"I don't want to, because there are no details. You act as though phones can't have glitches."

Gabrielle sighed. "Juliet, I know I saw that hair. . . . Those argan-oiled curls kind of stick out when everyone else is an unshowered backpacker."

"Fine. I was there by myself."

"You had a secret rendezvous with yourself? Oh, Juliet, you could do that in the comfort of your own bathtub. With the argan oil and everything."

Juliet laughed out loud, and felt relief. She could tell Gabrielle was starting to believe she hadn't been with anyone. "Shut up! I was at a *movie*."

"A regular movie?" Gabrielle asked. "By yourself?"

"Yes, why not?" Juliet said.

"For starters, your home theater is better than any screen in Paris."

"I know," Juliet said. "I just wanted to see something with a big crowd. Like normal people." At the mention of normal people, a few Metro riders flicked their eyes over her, as if wondering why she wasn't normal. Juliet quickly tried to remember the names of movies that were playing, but Gabrielle didn't ask.

"Ugh, you and your mad love of the proletariat," Gabrielle clucked instead. "Can't you at least *pretend* you were having a wild, passionate affair? You're so beautiful. You should be the subject of much better gossip."

Oh, I am, Juliet thought, turning her back on two twenty-something women who were glancing down at a fashion magazine and then looking at her like they knew her. "I'm sorry to have let you down again," Juliet said. "But I've got to go. If I don't let Maman know I'm on the Metro heading home, she'll send out hunting dogs."

"The Metro?" Gabrielle wailed. "You didn't even call a car?"

Juliet smiled to herself. The threat of Gabrielle gossiping

would be avoided now. Gabrielle lacked the imagination to believe Juliet would return from a tryst on the train. In the model's world, such encounters required cars and drivers afterward. "See you at the Palais Galliera ball?"

"I'll be dangling on the arm of today's photographer. It was the only way I could console him after delaying the shoot. Apparently, chasing after you cost him the five minutes of light that best accentuated my left breast."

"As an official representative of the House of Capulet, it's my professional opinion that your left breast looks lovely in any light."

"And this is why I love you, even if you are so well behaved it's sickening."

"Your right breast, however . . ."

"*À bientôt*, Juliet!"

Gabrielle clicked off and Juliet quickly dialed her mother, reinforcing the story that she had been at the movies alone and assuring Hélène she'd be home in mere moments.

"The movies? In a seat where millions have sat before you? You could have lice! Or worse . . ." The unspoken "worse" was a concoction of her mother's most haunting demons, all the things she'd pulled herself away from and covered beneath a veneer of wealth and breeding.

Juliet often, if not forgave her mother's snobbery, at least allowed for it because Hélène didn't actually enjoy it. Juliet wasn't sure her mother allowed herself to really enjoy *anything*, because she was so focused on the constant maintenance of outward perfection. It ended up that even when annoyed or angry at her mother, Juliet's overwhelming emotion toward her was pity. How awful it had to be to constantly worry you were being judged, and to constantly be judging yourself. It didn't make connecting with Hélène easy. Her mother wouldn't even tell stories from when she was Juliet's age. Her mother's own family had been well-off, but troubled (lots of addictive personalities, it seemed, and Hélène's father had died with a number of gambling debts that Maurice had paid off), and she no longer had contact with them— or anyone from her past, for that matter.

"I don't have lice, Maman," Juliet said as the man standing next to her inched a few steps away. "Next stop is me. I'll be home in a minute."

She clicked off just as Hélène screamed to Lu Hai to prepare a bath, extra hot. Juliet had been taking showers for years, as Lu Hai knew, but Hélène liked to think of her as a little girl who still had her hair washed with pitchers of warm water poured over her head. As the train rattled on, Juliet let her thoughts veer back to the afternoon with Romeo . . . and Jim. It was so odd to think he'd made her blush and shiver when they'd first met—silly even, given how they felt like old friends by the day's end.

Maybe not silly. Jim had smoldering eyes, and he looked at you like he could see right into your mind and unlock your secrets. So intense, but funny, too. And reckless. She'd never let on to Romeo, but she could still feel the pressure of being huddled behind Jim on the bike, her body flush against the ripped muscles of his back. His helmet had been damp with his sweat, and the dense scent of him—smoky and salty—still clung to her. She had to admit, she'd wondered what it would be like to be with him. Would his kisses be gentle or fierce? What would the contours of his chest feel like beneath her palms . . . or her lips?

Juliet laughed out loud, prompting more looks from her fellow passengers. That kind of wondering was harmless fantasy, like daydreaming about a movie star. Jim could run up to her right now, completely naked (which would probably confirm Juliet's mother's suspicions about the behavior of Metro riders), and offer himself to her, no strings attached, but Juliet would feel nothing but embarrassed for him. She'd found the man of her dreams in Romeo. A smile played on her lips as she remembered the feel of his body casually but protectively surrounding hers as they chatted with Jim. Even when they weren't physically together, she felt him there the same way.

She indulged in romantic reveries the entire way to her home. True, the giant columned, balconied, and filigreed facade looked more like a section of the Louvre than a private residence, but Juliet had never lived anyplace else. She trotted up the steps to the massive front door, pausing to pat one of the two stone lions that bared their teeth on either side. The one on the right was hers. The one on the left was Henri's.

She wished things were as simple for the two of them now as they had been when they were children. Here they were, Juliet hiding a love affair—even from Henri, her most trusted confidant. Meanwhile, her older brother had to always put on the show of being the perfect heir to the company. (That he'd almost lost the reins for his treachery was not yet public knowledge as Juliet's father worked his machinations to determine if her brother could still be the next heir to the company.) At this point, Henri was just doing his best not to be entirely excommunicated. Juliet was the only one who knew about the demons Henri was still fighting to control, just to keep the peace.

"Juliet!" Hélène's voice rang out within seconds of Juliet setting foot in the freshly polished marble foyer. Stepping into the velvety sumptuousness of the Capulet home was like camping out in a jewelry box. And while plenty of people could only dream of it, to Juliet it sometimes felt like a satin prison. "In the parlor!"

The parlor was her mother's room, layered in shades of pink and splattered with lace. Juliet found Hélène on one of the pink chintz sofas. An outsider would probably believe Hélène was already dressed for the evening's party, but Juliet knew the black cocktail dress, diamond necklace, and flawless makeup were just Hélène's daytime look.

Her mother's personal cook, Carina, a young but plump and tired-looking woman (all her mother's help shared a similar aura of fatigue), set a small pot of tea next to Hélène and instantly brought Juliet a glass of Vichy water. She smiled at Juliet and Juliet gave her a smile of her own, but didn't feel honest doing so. Something about returning from the afternoon's adventures made her feel even more cloistered by the constant attention than usual.

Juliet was about to sit in one of the mauve Louis XIV chairs when her mother raised a hand to stop her. "Don't sit, you haven't bathed yet." She held her nose to emphasize her disgust.

Juliet refrained from rolling her eyes. Like Hélène could smell anything. The room was so heavily fragranced by the cloyingly rose-scented candles Hélène favored that just walking in was like being suffocated by a funeral bouquet.

Hélène looked Juliet over from head to toe, and Juliet involuntarily crossed her arms over her chest as if to protect her secrets.

But her mother was all business. "You'll be meeting a date tonight," Hélène said, waggling a cautionary finger when Juliet was about to speak. "No refusals this time. You've been dateless at the last four events. A beautiful sixteen-year-old girl with no one on her arm. It's a tragedy."

"Oh, yes, it's clear I will die alone, a waste of your superior genes," Juliet said, annoyed. She caught her mother's wince on the word *genes*, but she wasn't sorry for saying it. The effect of Hélène being so tightly wound meant that Juliet couldn't even have a real conversation with her, and she sometimes acted like Juliet just existed as a pretty belonging she could control. Yes, Juliet loved Romeo, but she resented the notion that without a boyfriend she was somehow wasting herself. For all the things she couldn't stand about her father, at least he put some stock in her intellect. "So, who will it be?" she asked.

Carina edged past her, kneeling to pour Hélène's tea—facelift tea. French women were known to age gracefully without panicking to find new methods to stall the process. Though she'd not gone the surgical route, Hélène still subscribed to every myth and theory about other ways and means to keep herself from getting wrinkles. It was a safe addiction.

As Carina left, Serge and Patric entered and began styling and coiffing Hélène for the evening. Serge opened a large makeup kit while Patric began running his fingers through Hélène's tastefully blond tresses. Juliet tried not to groan as her mother leaned her head back and sighed with pleasure.

"Who is my date?" Juliet asked again.

Hélène smiled, more to herself than to Juliet. "Pierre."

Juliet caught Serge and Patric exchanging a knowing grin. The truth was, her mother loved Pierre because he—like her facelift tea—was a balm against aging. He was an utter suck-up who flattered Hélène at every opportunity. Pierre loved to talk about how Juliet and her mother could be sisters, and fawned over Hélène's beauty. She ate it up. Juliet had been set up with him several times, for casual dates, and she went obligingly. He was nice enough, and liked her. But tonight, to go with him to a party where Romeo would be, and where she'd be longing for her boyfriend, not Pierre, not ever Pierre—she just didn't want to go at all.

She grimaced. "Is he my date or yours?"

"For you, of course. Don't be silly," Hélène said. "And for whatever reason, he jumped at the chance. So go clean up, I know where you've been."

It took Juliet thirty panicked, startled seconds too long to realize Hélène was talking about the movies and the Metro, not Petite Asie or the cemetery.

"Lu Hai!" Hélène called. "Please come disinfect this child!"

"It's fine, Lu Hai! I'm on my way!" Juliet hollered back, eager to leave her mother's quarters.

"Make sure you wear your perfume," Hélène called as Juliet reached the door. "Pierre loves it." For anyone else, this would just mean whatever department store perfume they had on their dresser. For Juliet, it actually meant *her* perfume, Juliet by Capulet, a clean, sparkling fragrance developed expressly to "evoke her unique spirit." Juliet didn't know if she'd take it that far, but they had done a good job.

Agitated by the swift gear change from a Romeo date and wanton thoughts about the American to a dreaded appointment with Pierre, Juliet ran up the spiral staircase to her bedroom suite. She could already hear the water running in the shower and knew Lu Hai had it blasting at the pressure (intense) and the temperature (blazing) that Juliet liked best. The massive bathroom retreat was also outfitted with Juliet's favorite bath gels, shampoos, and conditioners, none of which smelled anything like Hélène's rose-aroma nightmare.

Lu Hai had no qualms about taking the blouse right off Juliet's back and swatting her affectionately on the bottom as Juliet shimmied out of her jeans and into the shower. If Lu Hai had her way, she'd still be in there with Juliet, dressed in a poncho and shower cap, standing just outside the water spray and washing down the little girl she'd nannied since Juliet's birth. Thankfully, when Juliet had put her foot down around her eleventh birthday, Lu Hai hadn't made a fuss, though she did still stay in the room while Juliet showered. Juliet didn't mind. The bathroom was large enough that Lu Hai could tidy up while chatting with Juliet through the steam. It was nice, too, to have Lu

Hai's help wrapping a thick heated Frette towel around her when she was done washing up.

Lu Hai waited until Juliet was luxuriating beneath a column of water before she casually called over the roar, "You have fun at the movie?"

"It was great," Juliet said, realizing that she still hadn't even figured out what movie to say it was.

"No doubt. I'm sure you picked a good one." The statement, made without probing into what Juliet might have seen, was Lu Hai's way of saying she knew there was no movie. Lu Hai always knew everything about Juliet without being told. After Juliet's first time with Romeo, Lu Hai had somehow been wise enough to draw a bath with jasmine oil, telling Juliet without question or judgment, "This is a good place for women to think." For all Lu Hai knew about her, though, Juliet knew nothing of her nurse (a term she'd started using for Lu Hai when she was nine and *nanny* seemed too babyish). The tiny, wizened old woman always laughed off Juliet's questions, saying her own past was far less interesting than Juliet's present.

Juliet had a strong feeling that wasn't true at all.

"Did I hear your mother say you'd be paired up with Pierre tonight?" Lu Hai asked. Her accent had a Cajun lilt, even though Lu Hai said she was from "somewhere in Indochina."

"I will," Juliet said.

"Such a sad voice when I ask about your boyfriend," Lu Hai clucked.

"My boyfriend?"

"You've been dating, what, three months now?"

"If by dating you mean 'watching him come over to flirt with my mom,' then sure, we're dating."

Lu Hai clucked her tongue. "That boy comes here for you, not your mother. He's just smart enough to know that family comes first. That's always true, even when you think it's not."

Juliet quickly wiped away a circle of steam from the glass shower wall. She half expected Lu Hai to be staring in at her accusingly, but the woman was bent over the sink, scouring it. Still, Juliet felt something foreboding in her words, and cranked the hot water to get rid of a sudden chill.

An hour and a half later, Juliet was dressed in a strapless black vintage Dior gown that she'd personally studded down each side with gunmetal rivets, giving the elegant silhouette a punk edge. Her dark hair was pulled into a loose chignon, with a few strands falling around her face. She was riding in the back of her family's limousine, on the way to the ball and to her date with Pierre. Her brother, Henri, rode in the seat across from her. He, like her, looked as if he were on the way to his doom.

She and Henri had been equals in their powerlessness ever since Henri had had his "missteps," as the family called them. Henri was still technically the heir, but with "contingencies"— mandatory treatment plans, monitoring of his social life. For her part, Juliet was safe from ever having to worry about taking over; years of misogyny on the Capulet board meant no woman had ever been put in charge. Besides, the whole thing was more trouble than she'd ever think it was worth. With all of the branches of the family represented on the board, there were always rumors and theories as to who really wielded power behind the scenes. Some of them were so crazy as to feature the Knights Templar, a secret society formed in the Middle Ages and believed by some to still be active from a secret location. (Not so secret: The vague neighborhood of their supposed "headquarters"—somewhere underground on Rue du Temple in the Marais—incited enough fear that it had become a joke that it was the ideal place for guys to get a prudish date to snuggle in close.) Juliet thought it was a silly legend. But even if it wasn't true, everything about dealing with the board and its politics seemed like the ballet recitals Juliet had been forced to dance in as a child: appearing before an audience she didn't want for a performance she wasn't interested in giving. Or at least she felt that way most of the time.

She thought if Henri did end up being denied his birthright, he should strike out on his own. But Henri was too undisciplined and spoiled for that. So he would do what they wanted and be who they wanted, and in return, he'd have the lifestyle he was used to, without the drugs. And Juliet understood. It was all he'd known.

But the addiction didn't just go away. The disease that fed it was there and always would be. Their mother, who came from a long line of addicts, knew this but swept it under the rug (or, more accurately, made others sweep it there for her). So far, Henri had managed, but Juliet knew there were moments when he almost succumbed. Much as she wanted to have faith in her brother, she knew he would someday. Just as she couldn't stop loving Romeo, Henri had his unfightable loves. Tonight, he'd be their puppet, put on the arm of a model and made to pretend he was the strong foundation of the House of Capulet, as their parents wanted. But if the board chose, they could decide upon a new successor, especially if pressed by the company's more fearsome backers. Juliet's own name had been bandied about in the press, but at home she was just a pretty face with the occasional good idea. There was a chance the company could even go to her cousin Thibeau, though even the more tenuous Henri would be a better choice, she thought. At least he had a heart.

"So, Pierre tonight?" Henri said, looking across the gulf of the limo's back seat at their parents, instead of at Juliet. "Sounds fun." His tone hit up against the somewhat icy atmosphere in the limo. Juliet's parents wanted their kids to be enthused about the gala, but neither Henri nor Juliet could hide their despair.

Hélène ignored his clipped words. "He takes such good care of Juliet," she said.

"They look nice together, too," Juliet's father, Maurice, said, from his spot next to Hélène.

Hélène wore a daring red Capulet Couture dress with a neckline that would challenge bodies decades younger than her own, but she pulled it off with ease. Next to Maurice's hulking frame, her slight figure almost disappeared in the seat.

"I want you to take some photos with him tonight," Maurice added. "You are a beloved face of the company, too, Juliet. You know the little girls love a love story."

Then if only they knew my real one, Juliet thought, her mind escaping to the afternoon with Romeo.

"And someday, when you two are married, you'll have a collection of photos together that started now. . . ." Hélène chimed in.

"You hear that, sister? Married." Henri couldn't hide his disgust. "She's sixteen." He practically spat at their parents.

"It's a joke," Maurice said. "I'm not selling off my little girl. But when she does find a mate, I know Juliet will act for the good of the business." Maurice leveled a glance at Henri. "Perhaps I didn't raise two failures."

Henri silently turned to stare out the window. There was no arguing with Maurice on such points when his mind was made up.

"Actually, I was eighteen when I married your father," Hélène said in a blasé way as she checked her lipstick—Capulet Red #17, fashioned expressly for her though Juliet thought she should get a new look. She was so self-absorbed sometimes that she returned to conversations long after their direction had turned.

"Then talk to me in two years," Juliet said. *When I will have already figured out how to run away with Romeo.*

Sensing Henri was about to say something more, Juliet squeezed her brother's arm. There was no need for him to be worked up on her behalf. He didn't deserve it and had his own woes.

Besides, they'd arrived. The limo pulled into the circular drive where arrivals were being let out. A plush violet carpet had been unfurled up the steps to the museum. At the top of the stairs stood Pierre, handsome and eager in his white dinner jacket. Pierre LeFevre III was the scion of an ancient noble family, and he carried off the whole aristocrat thing with aplomb. He had a swirl of dark hair and plump, almost girlish lips, along with a perfectly straight nose and a chiseled jaw. You could have made a Prince Charming cookie cutter using him as the mold, but Juliet didn't want Prince Charming. She wanted Romeo, and Pierre was no Romeo.

Juliet made her way up the stairs, smiling for photographers.

"Juliet, you look beyond gorgeous," Pierre said when she reached him. He took her by the arm and Juliet couldn't stop herself: She flinched.

Then her mother pinched her. Hard, just above the elbow. "He complimented you, Juliet," Hélène said. "What do you say?"

"Thank you, Pierre," Juliet said, hearing how stilted her voice was. "You look nice as well."

He beamed. It made Juliet feel sorry for him that he couldn't detect how hollow her words to him were. Instead, he guided her into the party, helping her to pivot for the sake of the photographers snapping shots of the entering guests. Juliet had little doubt that her smile failed to reach her eyes.

The museum had been transformed into a sumptuous party spot. The theme for the night was *Tout Est Possible*, or "Anything Is Possible"—ironic, Juliet thought, since one impossibility was her going with the date she actually wanted to bring. But it did indeed seem like the organizers had decided to do everything in their power to make the event a big deal.

The grand hall was a dazzling array of twinkling lights and soft draperies. The evening was a celebration of fashion through the ages, and mannequins wearing clothes from the Marie Antoinette era through the glory days of Coco Chanel lined the two staircases leading down to the main floor of the museum. A Capulet gown worn by Catherine Deneuve to the Oscars faced off with a famous Montague racing suit created for Paul Newman—the outfits were positioned so as to look ready for battle. Juliet wondered if it had been intentional.

Pierre placed a hand on Juliet's shoulder and she drew a sharp breath and cringed. "I need to find the powder room. Excuse me," she said, her voice rigid and formal.

"Of course," he said. "Return to me soon. I'll wait for you near the dance floor."

She stepped through a throng of people and started scanning faces for Romeo's. She did this often—at school, on crowded streets, always hoping she'd turn a corner and see him. It was hopeless, though. Even if she saw him, what could she do about it here?

Feeling overwhelmed, she made her way toward a darkened wing of the Palais, one not in use for the party. The lights were dim and the air had the comforting smell of an old building—a damp dustiness that was more a weight than a scent. She leaned against the cool brick, scanning an exhibit of old military uniforms that probably hadn't been updated in years. She knew she had to go back. Sighing, she pried herself away from the wall and turned . . .

Right into Romeo.

He wore an all-black tuxedo, his blond hair gelled back. His smile was electric; Juliet's heart clutched at the sight of it.

"You . . ." she breathed. How could she not believe their love was magical, when she'd wished for him and here he was?

"I had to get away," he said. "After today, it's awful to be with so many people who aren't you."

"I know," Juliet said, and she slid her hand into Romeo's. She pulled him to a bench in front of one of the displays. They sat down, legs touching. "Let's sit for just a minute. Hold my hand. And then you will go back to the party. And then I will. Until we can see each other again."

Romeo's smile was faint. "I'm always so happy when you say 'again.' "

"But it's never as soon as I wish it would be," Juliet said. She rested her head on his shoulder as he ran his thumb over her fingers.

He kissed her forehead lightly. "You have to look at it my way," he said. "We have what's most important. We just have to bide our time."

"I know," Juliet said, lifting her head. She didn't add how biding time meant missing all that they could have right now. She slid slowly along the bench, until they were at opposite ends, their hands still clasped at the middle.

"You should get back," she said, feeling the drop in her heart as she anticipated him leaving.

Romeo stood and helped her up. He pulled her in by the waist, like they were about to dance, and bent his head close to hers, so their lips nearly touched. Juliet put two fingers over his mouth. "Don't kiss me," she said. "Or we won't be able to stop."

So he kissed her fingertips, brushed his lips along the top of each one. "You're right. In every way," he said. "Just remember that what's out there isn't real. This is." And he left.

Juliet took a moment before she went back the way she came. If they were caught emerging from the same wing, all the work they had put into their assignations would be for nothing. So she stuck to the building's perimeters, taking her time to return to Pierre, who would be a floor below, on the dance floor beneath the museum's entry steps.

And yes, couples were already spinning across the dance floor, and already, Juliet found herself looking not for Pierre but for Romeo.

Again, she found him instantly, but this time her heart clutched in horror instead of delight. Romeo was locked in step with Rosaline Linara, a fresh young model recently hired as the face of the House of Montague. Declared "the anti-Gabrielle" by French *Vogue*, Rosaline was all Renaissance softness, compared to Gabrielle's modern, angular beauty. She had flowing dark hair and the kind of bright blue eyes that shocked you with their clarity. Her body, lithe but somehow just generous enough in the bust and hips, looked made for the flowing electric-blue Montague dress she wore. Happiness radiated off the girl as she twisted and twirled in perfect synchronization with Romeo. Other dancers stopped to watch the two of them together, and none of them could help but smile. Romeo and Rosaline looked like a perfect couple in love. It was heartwarming to all.

Juliet's stomach lurched and she thought she might pass out. How easily he went from holding her hand and feeling like hers to dancing in synchronized steps with Rosaline. *I thought it was so awful for you to be with people who weren't me,* she told him silently. She gripped a banister next to a mannequin in a vintage YSL jumpsuit. This, *this* was the kind of moment when Juliet wished she had a female friend to talk to, or that she could have Gabrielle reassure her that she was prettier, better than Rosaline. Much as she knew she had plenty to be grateful for, Juliet hated the Capulet way of distrusting everyone, and never revealing a true emotion to anyone outside the family.

"Are you all right?" Pierre asked, taking her hand. "You look pale."

"I'm fine," Juliet said, smiling while looking over his shoulder. Okay, she would have liked to confide in someone, but certainly *not* Pierre, even if he no doubt would ooze compliments to make her feel in every way superior to Rosaline. Ugh. "Would you like to dance?"

Pierre smiled with such joy that Juliet almost felt bad for him. "I'd love to," he said.

He led her by the hand to the dance floor just as the song ended. In the lull before the band began the next number, Juliet caught Romeo's eye. His gaze bounced off hers like she was no more than one of the mannequins. Or worse, a piece of furniture. She wanted to tear her heart from her chest.

Even if he was pretending, how did he do it so well? Wasn't he as tortured as she was? Did he just forget her as soon as they parted?

But of course he remembered. She knew he did. She knew that the little time they got together depended on them playing this indifference act to perfection.

But this was too hard and too cruel. She could still feel the warmth of his hand in hers.

The band launched into a slower song. Rosaline poured herself into Romeo's arms, clinging close as they swayed together. Juliet let Pierre pull her in closer. The room was a whirl of motion. Across the dance floor, Gabrielle's photographer was dipping her as Gabrielle's eyes zeroed in on Henri and his date, the new face of Chanel, a pale Scandinavian with black glaze around her frosty blue eyes.

Though Juliet felt Pierre's hand tight at her waist, the only other person on the dance floor, in the room, on the planet, was Romeo. Her entire being alighted on him, ached for him. Even as she moved in Pierre's arms, she subtly and slowly guided them toward the other couple. Though Romeo never looked her way or gave her any sign, he must have been doing the same. With every beat of the music, the two couples moved closer and Juliet's heart pounded faster. He was so close now, she could feel him, far more than she could feel Pierre's hands as they grasped her, or his breath as he lowered his head close to hers. When Juliet and Romeo finally brushed against one another, so softly, back to back, his touch rocketed through Juliet like a firecracker. She, who'd been trained to dance like this, stumbled on her heels. Pierre pulled her up straight, concern in his eyes.

"Are you okay?" he asked.

Juliet watched Romeo's retreating back, her breath coming shallow and fast. "I'm fine."

For the rest of the night, that slightest touch was their passionate kiss. The one she hadn't allowed to happen in the dark wing of the Galliera. It bound Romeo to her. No matter who he held, no matter who he danced with, no matter who he kissed good night, he was Juliet's.

"Excuse me!"

A burst of feedback squealed through the microphone, and all the dancing couples pulled away from one another and winced.

"Pardon." A smallish man with the carriage of someone much larger walked confidently across the stage. He was trim with a dour face but in such a precise way that you knew being trim and dour were his goals. He was standing in front of the band like he owned them. Like he owned the whole place.

"Pardon," he said, louder. "I don't mean to break up the party." But as he signaled to the band to stop playing, it was clear he entirely meant to break up the party. "Thank you," he said, his glinty eyes passing over the crowd as though everyone present

was a mere ant to him. "I'd like to thank *Maintenant* for giving me this venue and this forum to make a special announcement, seeing as they're the ones sponsoring this evening."

The room had gone quiet. Amélie Cardon, the editor of *Maintenant*, was famously controlling when it came to the magazine's events, so this man must have really been important for her to let him speak. "Hopefully, this won't take long to say." The accent was American, with a hint of something else that seemed familiar to her. Maybe a little Southern? She couldn't quite place it.

"I'm James Redmond. I think a few of you have heard of me," he said. Juliet felt she may have heard that name somewhere, but she was at a loss for who the man was. She was a reasonably informed sixteen-year-old girl, but she hardly stayed abreast of the who's who of American businessmen.

"This has been in the works for a while, but it only recently became appropriate for me to announce it. And I wanted to be the first to say something, so the fashion community didn't hear it elsewhere first." Here, he cleared his throat while staring over the heads of the "fashion community" to whom he was speaking. "I've been in many lines of business in the United States, but fashion is one area where I have no holdings. Quite frankly, I'm not even sure I know what I'm doing. Does this suit look okay?" He gestured to his obviously expensive but drab gray suit while chuckling at his own joke.

"So, to bring Redmond Industries onto the runway, I plan to purchase the two oldest houses in the game, the House of

Capulet and the House of Montague. It's been too long that they've been rivals angling for the top spot, so with my help, we'll unite them under one glorious banner. By next year, this ball will be celebrating *that* moment in fashion history."

The entire room burst into shocked gasps and murmurs. For just one second, Juliet's eyes found Romeo's and she saw in his face the same panic that surely showed on her own.

They'd both heard it: The American basically wanted to destroy their families. To him, he'd be turning the legacies of the houses into mere blips in the annals of American business. But for her and Romeo, it would be much more than just an entry on a ledger: It would be a death blow to their way of life.

Up on stage, beneath the silvery lights, James Redmond raised both his hands in the air to calm the vibrations of the crowd. "Please, please, know that there are still many threads to the story we need to tie together." He grinned and added, in surprisingly good French, *"Tout est possible. . . ."*

CHAPTER 6

JULIET

"WILL YOU BE OKAY?"

Pierre had asked her that same question every minute since the James Redmond announcement. The look that accompanied the question turned her stomach the most. His wide-eyed and urgent concern seemed weak.

"Am I dripping blood from a severed limb?" Juliet said, loud enough to be heard over the music, loud enough that a cluster of partygoers plucking hors d'oeuvres off a passing tray turned to look at her. She felt instantly bad for the sharpness in her voice.

But Pierre laughed. He had nice enough eyes, when they weren't infused with worry. She liked his hair, dark and floppy, as easy as he was. Pierre bore the air about him of a person who went happily into each day, never expecting chaos or turmoil. To her, that feature was by far the most irritating thing about him. "You have a dark sense of humor," he said. "It's very cute."

If Romeo had made the same comment, it would have delighted her, but from Pierre's lips—why were they always so shiny?—the words just made her cringe.

Juliet knew this wasn't good news. Not at all. A person would have to be an idiot to not have seen how quickly her father and Romeo's father, Jean Montague, had left the room, lacking all subtlety as they marched out, faces drawn, phones pressed to their ears. Being at a party to celebrate their companies' future in the presence of a man who was the business world's Grim Reaper defined irony. It may have been the first thing the Montagues and Capulets had ever agreed on.

Juliet's main concern was Romeo. After the announcement, Rosaline had snaked her arms around Romeo as if she would protect him from the threat of financial and familial ruin. And Romeo hadn't done anything to stop her. Juliet knew he couldn't exactly push her away, but she felt he should demonstrate at least a gentle rejection. Turning away from her instead of smiling at her might be a start. But his body language would have convinced anyone, Juliet included, that he was enjoying his date.

"It's bad news, though, for your family's company?" Pierre asked, and now he tried to put an arm around her shoulder. Juliet's arms involuntarily shrank into her sides. Why was it so easy for Romeo to be handled by Rosaline, when to Juliet, a touch from anyone else felt wrong?

"I suppose we'll find out," Juliet said. The party was still going on and most of the attendees had absorbed the news and continued with their joviality. It was different for her and her family, and probably for Romeo and his. Their families were their companies, and vice versa.

She wanted to talk to Romeo, to be alone with him behind the building, sharing a cigarette and making guesses as to how this all would play out. The news had left Juliet with a sliver of hope: If the Houses of Montague and Capulet were doomed by this outsider anyway, maybe it would also mean the end of all this silly rivalry that kept her and Romeo apart. She didn't want to have this thought, and felt guilty as soon as she did. But if this threat could mean losing everything her family knew—their house, the family vacations, the ease of life that came with never really worrying about money—then she could have Romeo, couldn't she? Hadn't she said she'd give it all up for him? And she would, she thought, but having everything taken from her family was different from leaving it all behind, and she couldn't feel good about her family's destruction.

As a tray carrying foie gras tarts passed her line of vision, Juliet feigned wanting one, and moved closer to Romeo and Rosaline, who'd been joined by several lesser models. If she could get his attention, maybe she could signal to him to meet her outside. The building was old, with plenty of nooks and crannies where they wouldn't be seen.

But before she could even reach the waiter, her father's large hand wrapped around her upper arm. "Come, *ma fille*," he said. "We need to leave."

The car was waiting for them out front. Pierre, perhaps in an attempt to ingratiate himself with the family, was leaving with them. Fortunately, Henri put himself on the seat between Juliet and Pierre. He leaned close and whispered into Juliet's ear, "Papa is looking afraid of the boogeyman, no?"

It was true. Their father, usually a stout and hearty man, was pale-faced as he got into the car. He may as well have been issued a death threat.

His phone rang and he pressed the button to answer, holding it tightly to his face. "Maurice Capulet." Her father almost never got phone calls—he called you, you didn't call him.

"Non, non," he said. Then he was listening, promising to be somewhere the next day.

"Oooh, the Knights Templar," Henri said under his breath with a snicker. He touched his Capulet signet ring to Juliet's. It was a long-standing gesture to their bond. They'd seen a brother-and-sister pair do the same thing in a French cartoon.

"The boogey*men*," she said back, wiggling her fingers. The joke was one they trotted out whenever their father was tense or in a bad mood, to blame the shadowy organization for his woes. As kids, they'd even played a game wherein they were on the run from the Templars (and of course their rings gave them the power to hide). Still, the joke had started to send a worried shiver up Juliet's spine ever since Henri's overdose. When they'd found

Henri (quite literally in the gutter), he'd been mumbling something about the Templars. The doctors had said he was probably delirious and acting out a game from childhood, but it still troubled Juliet.

"I think Papa must be feeling powerless," Henri said. "And we know how he hates that." Juliet couldn't tell if her brother felt a wee bit vindicated by this. She was gripped for a moment by one of those bursts of love for her family. She wanted to hug her father and assure him it would be okay. She wanted to tell her brother that he'd regret rooting against the family, even if things had been hard for him lately. But the thoughts were hypocritical, too, since just moments ago she'd been fantasizing about the freedom that might come from her family's failure.

Juliet shook her head. "Of course he feels powerless," she said. "That man just announced he was going to take over our company and our enemy's. To be reduced to the same level as a Montague must kill him."

She was desperate to ask Henri what he thought it meant, the companies being dismantled, maybe merging.

And that guilty thought came again, like a wave pulling her beneath the surface of things: What if a year from now the names Montague and Capulet meant nothing? Could that be exactly what she wanted for herself and Romeo?

CHAPTER 7

ROMEO

SCHOOL.

Romeo was the heir to a fortune and would one day preside over one of the world's great fashion houses.

But he still went to high school.

He attended Lycée Louis-le-Grand, like every other would-be success-story teenager in Paris. It was the school of Paris's writers, its scientists, its politicians, its *names*. Plus, it was in the Latin Quarter, the city's educational bosom, which meant that there were plenty of places to buy "study aids," as Benoit called them, from students paying their way through *université*.

Romeo could have bypassed school but he insisted on going. His father already thought he was incapable of being serious, so at least the day-in, day-out of school proved he had a discipline for something. And if he was going to go to school, it would be at Louis-le-Grand, not some remote boarding school far out of the city. (Even before Juliet, boarding school had held no appeal; all those women more or less trapped by the confines of a remote campus made them too eager. Where was the fun in that?)

However, even when Romeo thought he was doing the responsible thing, Jean Montague second-guessed the idea. Yes, the senior Montague, who had once read the definition of *uptight* and thought it sounded too playful, sometimes told Romeo that he could slide into the driver's seat of the House of Montague now, and learn on the job rather than waste time in class. But his fears about his son's character kept him from pushing Romeo to take the offer. Romeo knew these fears were due to the senior Montague's knowledge of how he himself had first operated as heir to the fashion house. When Jean had stepped into the role twenty-odd years ago, his hard-partying ways and endless parade of women had almost bankrupted the company. Shareholders wanted someone fashionable running the ship but not someone whose romances and brawls outshone the actual fashions. The weaknesses had all been exploited and exposed by the House of Capulet, which seized on the faltering moment as a way to gain the upper hand in the Paris fashion world.

It had taken years—and, Romeo was sure, the threat of being disowned—for Jean to turn his life around. It helped that he had somehow landed the glamorous but grounded Catherine Delaise, a model-turned-designer. The aristocratic background of the

Delaise name lent trust to the Montague name. Plus, Romeo's mom was capable of that thing certain girls had mastered: making you feel adored but also just uncertain enough of their continuing adoration that loving them was like a drug. Juliet could be like that. Every meeting with her, even though there'd been too few for his liking, Romeo always felt certain she wouldn't show. Then, when she did, it was better than any high he'd experienced.

It would be a lie to say that Romeo and his dad didn't "get" each other. Before his father reformed for his bride (and his stake in the company), he and Romeo lived similar louche lifestyles. But one thing Romeo got that his father didn't was that school kept him grounded, alert. Besides, after years of schooling with private tutors, Juliet had started attending Louis-le-Grand this year. Hate each other though they may, the Montagues and Capulets agreed on one thing: The best school in all of France was Louis-le-Grand.

Juliet's arrival had changed the air in the school. She'd for so long seemed almost a captive in the fortresslike Capulet manse, and then she was free, among the other children of Paris, though she was dropped off daily in a dark car with even darker windows.

Romeo had dismissed her as a spoiled princess before their first fateful meeting, but she had still been a presence to him. To everyone, really. To be able to look away from Juliet Capulet was to be something other than human, honestly. She was bewitching. Even Benny, hardly eloquent, had once said of her, "She's like magic, you know? You look and you look to try to figure out how she does it and finally you realize you're just as happy not knowing."

(Then he'd apologized. No Montague was ever to give credit to a Capulet.)

Now, Romeo pulled into his private parking spot. Most students took the Metro but he liked his freedom. And he liked to drive his black Lamborghini. On good days, he charged around the Arc de Triomphe a few times, gunning his engine just for the thrill. He may have wanted to be grounded, but he wasn't above enjoying some of a Montague's inherited perks.

Since Romeo had picked him up that morning, Benny had not stopped talking about the party the night before. Benoit wanted to know everything there was to know about Rosaline, Romeo's pseudo-date for the evening. Romeo knew that his cousin had witnessed James Redmond talking about the takeover, but it was in true Benny style not to bring it up. He had a gift for avoiding anything too hard.

"Just tell me what her ass feels like under your hands. Does it have push-back?" Benoit was talking rapidly but his attention was split as he looked out the window toward the sidewalk, ogling the passing *filles* of the Sixth Arrondisement's many posh schools.

"What?" Romeo wondered what his cousin was on today. Sometimes, he wanted to urge Benny to slow down, but he never knew if Benny would be contrite and actually listen or if he'd get defensive and go on a bender. In the past, it could go either way.

"Push-back," Benny said, putting his hands out in front of his face and simulating squeezing. "You press your hand into it and it rises up to meet your palm. The mark of a firm derriere. You just want to bury your face in it."

Romeo couldn't help but laugh at the enthused expression that accompanied the crude joke. "My friend, the reason you don't have a woman in your life is because you think of women in terms of body parts," he said.

"What, are you a feminist now?" Benny asked, with real concern. He slung his Hermès messenger bag over one shoulder and slid the car door shut. "Is that what happens when you've been through all the women in Paris? You start looking out for their feelings?"

"Rosaline was . . . nice," Romeo said, hoping to convey enough false bravado with his grin so that Benny could imagine whatever scenario Benny wanted to imagine. Rosaline was perfectly nice, and beautiful, but she lacked that *je ne sais quoi*—that Julietism—to make her what he needed.

"I'll bet," Benny said, in the wistful tone of a guy who lived through another guy's dates. Which Benny did. "So, you worried? About that American fuck?"

Romeo looked at Benny. He'd not expected this. Was talking about Rosaline's ass Benny's, ahem, backdoor way of bringing this whole thing up?

"What? The Redmond guy?" Romeo tried to act casual. The truth was, he knew it was a big problem. He also knew he did not want to deal with the whole school eyeballing him like his entire family had just died. Still, he was prepared for just that to happen. No business, no money—if it really came to pass, he might as well be dead to everyone he knew. "No."

He was lying, and about to elaborate on the falsehood.

But a bike that pulled up to the corner across from the school caught his eye. A Richard Pollock bike. A custom-built Mule with a set of shiny chrome exhaust pipes, stretched long like a woman's legs; its vintage design contrasted with the Mule's very modern speed. Romeo couldn't help staring; the machine was a beautiful thing. He felt the way Benny probably did asking about Rosaline—like he wanted to know the exact feeling of the bike and its pleasures.

The rider hopped off and lifted the helmet from his head. It was . . . Jim. The dude who'd pulled Romeo and Juliet out of yesterday's jam. What was he doing here? And how many exotic bikes did he have? Romeo thought the American had been exaggerating yesterday. That's what those guys did. But no, here he was with a Mule.

A minute ago, Romeo had felt the same blasé indifference toward the day as he always did when he wasn't going to be alone with Juliet. Now, he grew instantly tense and sweaty under his just-rumpled-enough shirt (only the unwealthy fretted over being extra-pressed). Romeo was never tense and sweaty. But this guy knew about him and Juliet. And it appeared he was now attending Louis-le-Grand. So he'd be under the same roof, day in and day out.

Jim's look of recognition was subtle. Still, to a loyal friend like Benny, it was enough.

"You know this dude?" Benny whispered under his breath. His hackles were already up. If he could fight on Romeo's behalf, he would. Gladly.

"Yeah, a little bit. Through my mechanics," Romeo said, hoping he was loud enough for Jim to hear, so he'd back up the lie. With another admiring look at the bike, Romeo added, to Jim, "Bike's looking good, man. You got a second?"

Now Benny gave the bike an appraising look, then glanced at Romeo, as if to say, *You need me?*

"This guy's got a vintage Triumph I've been meaning to ask about," Romeo said. He didn't know if it was true, but it sounded good. "Go ahead without me, Ben."

Benny nodded and headed toward the main gates of the school. He looked back once as if to remind Romeo that he had his back if Romeo needed him. Romeo hoped he wouldn't.

"What are you doing here?" Romeo asked, drawing himself to his full height. He was taller than the American, but Jim's shoulders did that thing where they pressed into the back of his jacket. It wasn't something he normally paid attention to, but Romeo was still feeling twitchy about the fact Juliet had leaned into this guy's back less than twenty-four hours ago.

"You said you'd call, but I know how that works. Guys never call," Jim said with a giant grin. Asshole looked like the spokesperson for the rare and ultrafast motorcycle he was leaning against. And Romeo wasn't the only one who noticed. Every girl passing by did a double take. Girls Romeo had bedded looked from him to Jim like the new stranger in town might be exactly what they'd need to forget that Romeo had done them wrong. And for his part, Jim was just nonchalant enough to give them the most passing of passing glances. Dude had game.

At the very least, a new guy distracted from Romeo's business news enough that fewer people gave him "sucks to be you" grimaces than he thought would.

It kind of bothered him.

"Come on, dude," Jim said. "I go to school here now. It's my first day. Ten years, fourteen boarding schools. Make that fifteen now. But maybe I won't get kicked out of something public. And French." He watched as a brood of black-clad girls swish-hipped their way past. They were Les Unimpressed, as Benny liked to call them, because they never looked his way, but each one looked at Jim and each one offered her own version of a come-hither smile. "Or at least I'll try not to." Jim grinned back at the girls. But it was a smile Romeo had delivered a time or two: It meant the female attention was of little consequence to him. His grin said, *There are always more where you came from.* Romeo knew that grin because he himself had perfected it.

He didn't care, of course. He had Juliet. He loved Juliet.

But who did this Jim think he was?

"I didn't know you were a boarding-school kid," Romeo said. He held open the tall wrought-iron gate that led to the school's front courtyard, facing Rue Saint-Jacques. Students milled about, finishing takeaway cups of coffee while hovering over smartphones, furtively puffing Gitanes, Camels, and Gauloises in corners nestled away from the front doors.

Now he could feel the examining gazes returning his way. His classmates had two reasons to size him up today: The idea that a golden boy like Romeo might lose everything with this takeover scenario was juicy gossip. Plus, he was walking around with a new American kid.

Jim shrugged. "Yeah, I try not to wear my pedigree like a country club blazer. Leave it to the other men in my family to do that. Full name is Jim Gardner. And my guess is you're not Benedict."

On cue, a few guys from the lacrosse team yelled to Romeo, "Montague, does this takeover mean you won't be Côte d'Azur–ing with us on winter break?"

Romeo swiped the air with his hand, like he was clearing it. "Come on, like James Redmond can really take down the biggest fashion label in Paris."

Christian Torrant, one of the forwards, shrugged arrogantly. Romeo had always hated him. "Sounds like he's taking down you *and* Capulet. But she'll go down prettier."

His cocky grin made Romeo want to slug Christian in the face. Instead, he gave him the finger and turned back to Jim.

"Yeah, not Benedict. Romeo Montague is my name," Romeo said. Then, looking around, he spoke in a whisper. "And Beatrix, the girl you met me with, she's really Juliet Capulet. And yes, I fucking hate what that prick just said about her." Yesterday, he'd been so glad for the aliases Juliet had crafted, but it was pointless to keep up the ruse now. Jim would find out their real names. Romeo guessed that the guy would be like most Americans, though—unconcerned with the bold-faced names of French fashion. "Just don't say you saw us together. I'm not supposed to be with her. She's not supposed to be with me. No one can know."

They were walking through the front doors now, and Jim unzipped his jacket to reveal the same kind of tight T-shirt he'd had on yesterday. Romeo had always been lean and suddenly felt self-conscious about it. Jim had that boxer build that Romeo knew to call a boxer build because it had been key for the Montague men's line last fall.

"Yeah, I kind of figured that," Jim said coolly as he glanced around the hallways of the old building.

Romeo found the American's easy way about the situation infuriating. "How would you know that?"

"You don't think the tip-off would be having to sneak you out of a bar like two fugitives? It's not every day a future captain of industry flees the scene scrunched down in my sidecar."

Even more infuriating. Mostly because he was right.

"What do you mean, 'captain of industry'?" Romeo said. Now his hackles were up.

Jim waved off the question. "Nothing to be ashamed of. Look, you and some model are all over the blogs this morning. I don't even read that crap most of the time, but you're everywhere today. Even if I was just some Joey T-Shirt American, I'd probably notice you guys."

Romeo didn't really want to be reminded about the inescapability of the Rosaline images. They were everywhere, and he knew Juliet must have seen them. She had nothing to worry about. He'd been playing a part, thinking the whole time of how perfect it had been to hold Juliet's hand in that dusty room of the museum. But a photo could make a person's mind wander. And one of the things he loved about Juliet was her ability to imagine whole other lives for them. He could see how that quality could turn on him.

"So, you going to need a tour guide?" Romeo asked, changing the subject. He was jealous of the way the American glanced around without giving off the slightest sense he might be nervous about his new school, or about anything . . . that was supposed to be *Romeo's* attitude. "Someone to make sure you know the ropes?"

"What is this, a TV movie?" Jim asked, smirking at a third-year girl with shiny raven-colored hair. "I've got a schedule and a map."

Jim talked like he didn't care about a guide, but he didn't seem to hate following Romeo to his locker, which was in the school's east wing. It was the same hallway where Juliet's locker was stationed, but she was never as early as Romeo. He lingered some mornings, for the chance to see her walk in. If the halls were especially crowded, they might make brief, secret eye contact.

Just as he was thinking about this, she arrived. Her friends Catrine and Margaux flanked her. Juliet wasn't close with the girls, but she'd been besieged with offers of friendship from the day of her arrival.

He saw, as she passed, the flick of her eyes over him and Jim.

Her soft brow furrowed slightly and the sweet frown he loved appeared. Romeo knew she must be wondering what Jim was doing here. He hoped the sad look on her face had nothing to do with the Rosaline photos.

Romeo grabbed his books and shut the locker, watching but not watching as she walked away.

"You don't say hi," Jim said. "That's sad. But, again, I figured."

"What, because of the model?"

"Geez, you forgot squishing yourself in my sidecar to protect your secret relationship already? I was hoping it would be a traumatic memory for you," Jim said.

Romeo couldn't help it. He laughed. "I'll make it one," he said. He hated to admit it, but he felt a relief around Jim that he'd never felt with Benoit, even if the latter was one of his oldest friends. He knew it was because Jim knew about him and Juliet. But how comfortable could he let himself be?

He looked at Jim with what he hoped was a serious expression. "Look, Juliet and I . . . obviously, well, it's not easy. And even though I'd love the world to know, it's beyond complicated."

Jim shrugged. "Bet it's not that complicated. Your families hate each other, right? And the old people figure if they keep the young people apart, it keeps their war raging. You're pawns."

Romeo nodded. This guy really got it. "What's your family business?"

"Hostile takeovers," Jim said with a laugh. "Heavy on the hostile."

"Sounds like you could be part of my family," Romeo said.

"Rich kids are all part of the same family, aren't we?" Jim pulled a slip of paper from his back pocket and looked down at it. "We have it good, don't get me wrong. But it's not like it looks from the outside. Seems like there's a price we pay for having money."

Romeo nodded. He wondered if he'd ever get to stop paying that price, or if all the promises he made to Juliet were hollow.

Jim patted his shoulder. "Anyway, I'm not saying a word. It's a special kind of dysfunction, ain't it?" Catching himself, Jim grinned. "Sorry, my last roommate was a good ol' boy whose dad did oil-field stuff. Sometimes I sound like him. I need to brush up on my French. I'll start in this next class, if I find it."

He walked off, lifting a hand to wave as he did so.

Romeo caught himself wondering when he would see him again, even as he knew he should stay away from him. Jim knew his biggest secret. But Romeo found himself thinking maybe it was okay to let one person know.

No, Romeo didn't want to like Jim, but he did. Romeo had a thing, it seemed, for liking people he wasn't supposed to.

CHAPTER 8

JULIET

IF SHE AND Romeo were a normal couple, this Monday would be a normal Monday. She could, like any jealous girlfriend, fling in her boyfriend's face that he'd gotten too cozy with another girl over the weekend.

Even if Rosaline was just business, Romeo had looked like he was taking some pleasure in the moment. Juliet had been fearful at the gala itself, but it was made even worse this morning, when she'd been scouring the gossip blogs. The worst: Romeo's hand on the small of Rosaline's back as they slipped out of their limo into Le Petit Marché. Rosaline leaning toward Romeo, whispering something into his ear with one hand possessively clamped on his sleeve.

The images conveyed the kind of close intimacy that Juliet imagined existed between her and Romeo. But it wasn't like *she* had any photos of them together to prove it to herself.

Funny how it was just so easy to take a single moment between Romeo and Rosaline and imagine an entire romance for them, with the same detail she'd used for her own visions of life with Romeo. It was an ability unique to females, she thought, to imagine not just an instance, but *everything*. Gabrielle concocted fantasies about her crushes—whole lifetimes—as soon as she met them. (And Gabrielle, Juliet knew, could take one morsel of a glance from Henri and imagine it meant something fateful between them. Gabrielle's capacity for denying the obvious—Henri liked but didn't love her—was another womanly ability.) Did men do the same thing? It didn't seem like it. Not from the way Romeo told her she was being silly to dream of escape. Not even, it seemed, from the way he didn't seem to realize how her mind would interpret the photos from the night before.

She was a mess this morning, moving as though in a fog, her body a clatter of anger and urgency. She wanted to rage against Romeo for his attentions to Rosaline. She also thought how she might need not rage if it weren't for fate, keeping them from just being Romeo and Juliet. Then there would be no Rosaline.

Life—even in a mansion right in the bud of the beautiful Avenue Montaigne—was not fair. When you grew up rich and privileged, you were prone to think that it was more than fair to you. But it found a way to take something from you, didn't it?

Lu Hai had noticed Juliet's existential funk that morning.

"Last night was not everything you wanted it to be?" She was shaking her head as she brushed Juliet's hair. The hair-brushing wasn't part of the normal routine anymore, but Lu Hai seemed to know what Juliet needed as she sat like a lump at her vanity.

Besides the obvious problems, this was what bothered Juliet about their secret relationship: What could she honestly ask of him? For that matter, what could he ask of her? Their relationship was just stolen moments in hidden rooms. Divine moments, yes, but as ephemeral and wispy as the way Juliet believed in a divinity. Sometimes the sun seemed to shine out from the center of every flower in the Jardin du Luxembourg . . . and it was easy to think a god had done it. But then the rest of the time, even in Paris, everything felt so humanly mundane that it was just as easy to forget the divine moment had ever occurred at all.

Was Romeo just a dream? A drug?

No, she couldn't march up to him between classes now and, with fire in her eyes, ask why she'd seen pictures of him leaving a late night dinner with Rosaline. (A dinner where the lithe model had no doubt smoked much and eaten nothing, not that Juliet was such a stranger to that diet.)

She was late for her French literature class but her mind was such a blur that she was fumbling through her locker, pulling out the wrong books again and again.

"*Merde*," Juliet huffed, finally finding her Balzac and slamming the locker shut. The halls had emptied. Catrine and Margaux had left her alone after making a fuss over the takeover news— "Does this mean you won't get free clothes anymore?" Catrine had asked, like an idiot. And then Juliet had refused to talk about Pierre, annoyed that her so-called friends couldn't understand why she wouldn't like a real LeFevre. She just felt bad for him, being so happy in her presence last night when her desires were so firmly elsewhere.

She never wanted to be where she was anymore, except when she was with Romeo. Her heart tugged angrily away from her body all the time now. She was distracted in school, depressed at home, and felt a hole inside her that wouldn't be filled if she couldn't have him. Her enviable life was spiraling out of control.

And then what she'd just seen in the hallway. Was it a hallucination? Or had Romeo really been standing there with the American from yesterday? She was in the dark as to what it meant. All her anger toward Romeo had fused with a fresh confusion and, if she admitted it, guilt. Yes, Juliet felt guilty. Guilty because when she'd woken this morning, it was with the fuzz of a dream in her head, and the fuzz—if she allowed herself to smooth it out—was from a *belle rêve* in which she was on the back of the motorcycle again, the lights of Paris far behind her and a wide expanse of ocean ahead of her. And also ahead of her were the shoulders she remembered from yesterday, encased in the black leather jacket she'd seen on Jim again today.

In sleep, her mind had gone to Jim, even though awake, she craved Romeo.

Her guilt over a dreamed dalliance was screwing up her fury at Romeo's real indiscretion.

She rushed down the hall toward her first class, almost tripping though she wore low-heeled boots along with a vintage Chanel skirt and a half-tucked old button-down of Henri's—another one. (Though she was the unofficial face of the House of Capulet, Juliet was also known for her effortless street style, a fusion of new and vintage pieces.)

"Damn!" She was so out of sorts she seemed capable of only one-word curses. Why should she feel bad about a dream—a dream that meant nothing? (Or, if it meant anything, it was probably her subconscious also being angry at Romeo for not agreeing to run away. Whereas Jim seemed like just the type to say yes without a second thought.)

She was angry at Romeo. That was all the dream signified. She wanted him to run away and Jim represented her wish for freedom. (How very American, no?)

As she rounded the corner in a hurry, two hands reached out and grabbed her by the shoulders.

"Whoa, hold up there," came a voice immediately familiar. An American accent.

Juliet looked up into Jim's coffee-colored eyes. They jolted her to earth like they were caffeinated.

She felt color rising in her cheeks. Could dreams be broadcast across foreheads, like replays of soccer matches?

"Hey, it's you," he said, *en anglais*. "Juliet." He said it hesitantly, watching her face almost like he wanted to make sure it was okay. His voice was soft and less assured than the day before. And was it her imagination or was he blushing a little, too?

"How do you . . ." Juliet's own English was fair but her voice trembled. Had they made an awful mistake, letting this American help them?

"Benedict told me," he said, in French now. Juliet took a second to process who "Benedict" was, but when she did, she felt her mouth pull into an O of surprise. Jim's eyes softened, the skin at the corners crinkling as he smiled down at her. Touching the top of her arm, he said, "Don't worry, my lips are sealed about you and Romeo."

His hand on her arm was warm and she caught herself looking at his face for far too long. Jim was someone who invited closer inspection. Juliet detected something beneath the swagger, as was usually the case. Most of all, she sensed she really could trust him.

"Well, who knows if there's anything to keep your lips sealed about?" Juliet said, dropping a step back and out of Jim's reach. A day when she was mad at Romeo was no time to be standing so near someone who'd featured in her dreams the night before. Not that she was honestly tempted, but she didn't want Jim to seep further into her subconscious.

Jim laughed. "You have to be kidding me. Is this about the model in the pictures?"

"What, you're on his side?" Juliet started down the hallway at a fast clip. Who was this stranger to come weigh in on her relationship problems? Or her problem relationship, as the case might well be.

Jim walked just as briskly as she did, or at least his stride was longer and he had little problem keeping up. "There are no sides," he said. "That guy is in love with you. Whatever was up with the model thing yesterday is pure publicity."

Now Juliet stopped. "Did he tell you that? She's just 'publicity'? Of course that's what he'll *say*," she said. "But that's not what I *saw*."

Jim hung his head down, like he was taking responsibility for the Rosaline incident, and for all men in general. "Let's put it this way," he said. "I'm a cocky American. And when I see a girl like you, nothing in the world would stop me from hitting on her, even if she had a boyfriend."

"*Charmant,*" Juliet said. Had she just been giving this guy credit for running deep two seconds ago?

Jim held up a hand and that cocky American grin returned. It was such a contrast from Romeo's more still intensity. There was something in the way Romeo looked at her that made her feel liquid, and like he could drink her all in. Whereas Jim made her feel like he might throw her over his shoulder and cart her off for more playful amusement.

"Gimme a second to get to the point," he said. His eyes were trained on hers, like he really wanted to be taken seriously. "I would hit on her *unless* I could tell so easily that she was in love with a guy who loved her back. And that guy leaves no doubt that he loves you back. Believe me. I hate admitting when I'm outmanned."

Juliet smiled at the sweet, shy way he said this. Why, sometimes, with Romeo and now with Jim, did she feel so much wiser, like she understood more, even if her experience in the world was more limited? Romeo called her a crazy dreamer when she spun tales of their running away, but some piece of her knew that her ideas were wholly sane. And now here was Jim, and she knew that he harbored some loneliness beneath all his bravado. Maybe she was wrong, but why did boys hide so many truths from themselves?

"Well then," she said, feeling a friendly affection for the American, "I suppose I should listen to you. Out of sympathy, at the very least."

Jim smiled. "It's the least you can do," he said. He held out his class schedule for her to see. "And maybe walk me to class. I'm lost, and you're the only one I'm willing to admit that to."

"Of course," Juliet said, thinking maybe Jim wasn't so unaware of his truths after all.

CHAPTER 9

JIM

FRENCH GIRLS.

Wasn't there a song about them?

No, that was "Some Girls." The Stones.

But there had to be a song about French girls. Especially about ones like Juliet.

Though he had a feeling that Juliet was the only girl like Juliet, French or otherwise.

First days of school. He'd done a lot of them. He liked them. They were fresh starts, as trite as that was.

By the time he arrived at one, another first, he usually really needed the fresh start. He'd have left behind a string of fed-up teachers, heartbroken women, and guys who were sick of losing those women to him. He wasn't even trying to be some prototype of a bad boy, but people sort of expected it from him, so that's what he gave them. It was easier than figuring out what he wanted to be.

But this time, with Romeo and Juliet, it was different. They weren't part of the usual fawning crowd of students who knew Jim's dad was James Redmond, the biggest shark in an ocean of sharks whose calling was eating alive the others like they were minnows. He might have been the newest of new money, but even the oldest of legacy students would suck up to Jim the second they heard. Anyone with any ambition wanted an in with the Redmond family and its fortune, and Jim was the new-school easy target. But Romeo and Juliet seemed to him like people who had bigger concerns than wealth. They were real potential friends.

Still, he'd meant what he said to Juliet. If not for Romeo, he really would have hit on her. No, no, not *hit on*. A girl like Juliet was worthy of something better. She was someone you *approached*. And *saw*. And *recognized*. She wasn't just another unimpressed fashionista. She was restless and searching, like him. Like Romeo, too, really.

Maybe he was wrong, but he didn't think so. Something about two teenagers who could date anyone they wanted choosing each other, even if it meant they risked their fortunes, it just seemed real. And right now, for reasons he didn't want to think about, Jim needed something that felt real.

Some rich kids were vapid and just took all their blessings without seeing that each one was its own curse. But Romeo and

Juliet weren't like that. Maybe eons of feuding families could do that to a person.

Yesterday, in the cemetery after he'd helped them escape the bar, it was the first time in years that Jim felt like maybe life meant something. Or, if it didn't, that at least there was something to be said for enjoying its finer moments.

What was France doing to him? Any second now he was going to be wearing a beret and quoting Sartre. Though who knew what that damn guy said?

Ha, philosophy, as if that would impress his dad. James Redmond didn't have patience for philosophy, unless there was a dollar figure and a bottom line attached. Jim had always thought that his dad's wheels spun for more than just money and power, but now he could see that those were the fuel in James Redmond's fire. It was the first time in years that Jim had been in the same city as his dad, and when they were far apart, Jim used to imagine his father having an eventful life of delights (wine, women, songs). In truth, what Jim was witnessing was that his dad worked nonstop. Or at least that's what he'd observed after interacting with him almost daily.

Okay, so *interacting* was a generous term—but only if you compared Jim and his father to other father-son pairs. Since his mom had died (fine, killed herself) when Jim was eight, he and his dad saw each other a few times a year, usually in breakfast meetings set up by whoever was his father's assistant at the time. The last three Christmases, James Redmond would have his staff send Jim details on his gift—a new car or motorbike—then appear on Skype to wish him a nice holiday in a session set up months in advance and lasting only five minutes, just long enough for Jim's fake joy to wear off by the end of it.

So, he was hopeful about being in the same metropolitan area as his father. He hated how desperately he wanted his father's approval—God, it didn't even have to be approval; Jim was contenting himself just feeling less like some annoyance James Redmond had to handle and more like someone who could at least share his dad's rarefied air. Yeah, that was a little dramatic, but feeling your father's utter indifference your whole life made you a little crazy.

And now his dad actually had a use for him. A business use, it seemed, but it was better than nothing. James Redmond was, above all things, an opportunist. At first, when Jim got kicked out of boarding school just as his dad was about to go to Paris to stage a takeover of two of the world's largest fashion houses, James Redmond didn't see an opportunity. He was just angry. His son's personal problems—your mother's suicide and father's neglect would do that to you, not that Jim was complaining (who would listen?)—were a massive inconvenience. Maybe even a hold-up of work to be done.

But then Jim had said, "Can't I come to Paris with you? Isn't there something I could do there? To help you?" Usually, he tried to never need anything from his father, but he was running out of boarding schools to try and, quite honestly, thought he'd feel less lonely in a city somewhere, instead of yet another bucolic and remote campus.

Jim's offer had revealed a whole new James Redmond. He'd never seen Jim as anything more than a burden, but now, suddenly, James had been reminded that his son was a human being capable of . . . something. Maybe Jim was just a pawn. But at least his father wanted to have him around.

James had his people determine Paris's best school and enroll Jim in Louis-le-Grand. The last name—Gardner—was his mother's maiden name. They'd discussed all these details on the plane ride here—his father ticking off various orders with military precision—as Jim nodded in agreement. He'd been amazed that his dad would even bother with him after yet another school failure. And then James had delivered the main thrust of his marching orders: "Keep an eye on this Romeo and Juliet," he had said.

Jim had been hoping for a job scouting models, but this was almost more interesting. And weird.

"What kind of stuff do you want me to find out?" Jim had later asked, after a few days in Paris that he'd spent wandering aimlessly, not really sure how to trail a person. He and his father had been dining at Le Relais de l'Entrecôte, a steakhouse on the Rue Marbeuf where the servers simply asked, "Medium or rare?" and brought you a plate of steak and *pommes frites*. The meal was James Redmond's favorite in all of Paris. He was not inclined toward gastronomical adventures.

James Redmond shook his head and swirled his Scotch—he only ordered wine if it was for someone else. With a slight smile, he told Jim, "As much as you possibly can. I have faith in you."

That little vote of confidence, however cliché, had given Jim the charge he needed for his assignment. If he could just prove to his father that he was useful, maybe something would come of it. He'd tracked Juliet from her house yesterday to the Love-Lock Bridge, then to that hotel in the Thirteenth. He hadn't expected Romeo and Juliet to come into that bar, or to need an escape.

The whole thing had been so absolutely surreal that he was shocked he hadn't somehow revealed his secret. Whatever kicked in—maybe years of half-assed attention paid to spy movies or maybe some kind of ability for subterfuge innate to being a Redmond—clued him in that seeming like their ally was the best way to gain insight.

Jim knew it was huge that they were a couple. He knew he'd had some kind of insane Paris luck to stumble on them in such a compromising position.

He could have snapped a photo on his phone. He'd have had the needed confirmation and been done.

But no. Something told him to help them. They'd been so panicked. Instinct had taken over. And then, as they rode with him on his bike to the cemetery—he always liked finding the cemeteries anywhere he was living—he thought he might be committing the ultimate subterfuge.

Maybe he was good at subterfuge.

But so far, he'd only lied to his father about the meeting. "I don't know if you're right. Juliet was out with some friend of hers all day yesterday," Jim had said as they'd poured coffee together at the counter that morning. His dad had been out late the night before because of the gala. (Jim had half-wished he could go but hadn't pressed his dad for an invite. He knew it could screw up his spy duties.) So, this morning, James was doing all his conference calls from home. While they had servants, James Redmond was big on being at least a little DIY. He liked to pour his own coffee, black, in the morning and stand at the counter with all the papers spread around him. "But I'll keep trying."

"You're tailing her?" James Redmond raised an eyebrow. "That was more than I'd expected from you."

Then he'd smiled. Jim wasn't sure if his father had really smiled at him in, well, ever.

He liked being good at his job. He also wished he didn't like Romeo and Juliet so much. He'd gone from feeling like someone with no loyalties to someone with divided ones.

Today, he'd gone straight home after school. It was weird, living with his dad again. Even in the summers away from boarding school, he'd been pawned off on friends to stay in summer homes and beach mansions while his dad worked.

Now he was under the same roof, in a penthouse on Avenue du Président Kennedy. (James Redmond wasn't crazy about being on a street named after a Democrat, but he did love that his penthouse had a coveted view of the Eiffel Tower.)

It was a nice place—no, "nice place" was what you called a bachelor apartment where the guy had a real bed and not just a mattress on the floor. This was a spectacular place. It was some kind of cross between the Palace of Versailles and Andy Warhol's Factory.

Most of the time, Jim had it all to himself. Right now, he was sprawled on the low red modern couch playing Assassin's Creed on the massive flatscreen. Bottles of French beer were scattered across the ornate ivory coffee table (everything in the penthouse was old "juxtaposed" with new, as the interior designer who stopped by with new old junk every week kept reminding him as she left a bill on the credenza).

What was he gonna do? On the one hand, he'd made a promise to his dad.

On the other, he already felt a loyalty to his new friends.

He was kicking the crap out of some horrible new boss, even though he couldn't remember getting to the end of his level. His movements were rote and automatic. He didn't really care about the game. It just kept him from thinking.

"Oh, you're home," came a breathy female voice. Jim's shoulders pulled up near his ears, like he was a turtle trying to go back into his shell.

Jennifer Reynolds, his father's chief of staff, looked like she'd stepped out of the Playboy Channel and had bought a Take Me Seriously wardrobe set. She wore tailored business suits and oversized glasses and her shiny blond hair was pulled back in a harsh bun. But very little could detract from her boat-show-model looks.

It was unfortunate, really, that her biological attributes had aligned the way they did. She was smart.

He knew his dad was screwing her, though whether it was a matter of the heart or just something James Redmond did to keep in fighting and corporate-downsizing shape, Jim didn't know. And for her part, Jennifer did a more than admirable job switching between cooing girlfriend and terrifying second-in-command.

Except, whenever they were alone, Jim felt like she was . . . seducing him. She wasn't really much older than him, so it wasn't that odd that she'd think he'd be interested in her. But he was living with his dad, and on speaking terms with his dad. Somehow, bedding his girlfriend/assistant/what-have-you didn't seem like the way to keep things on good terms with him.

Jennifer loosened her hair and plopped down on the couch next to Jim. She kicked off her shoes and stretched her tanned legs out on the coffee table.

"How was school?" she asked. She pointed at the TV. "You don't need to stop playing for us to talk."

Jim relaunched the game and this time, tried to focus. If he did, maybe Jennifer would go away. Next to him, Jennifer pulled her feet up onto the couch. Her red toenails brushed his jeans.

"Good, better than boarding school," he said. Jim realized his game controller had slipped from his hands because now Jennifer's bare feet were almost in his lap. He scooted over on the long couch, wondering if Romeo had to contend with such weirdness. Probably, though he'd bet a Frenchwoman would play things with more subtlety.

"I know your dad is happy to have you around," Jennifer said. She placed a casual hand on Jim's thigh and patted. It wasn't unpleasant. Not at all. And normally, he would love a buxom blond shamelessly flirting with him. But the whole point of being here was to share some time with his father. He didn't think sharing the same woman was part of the deal.

"Yeah, I just need to stay out of trouble," Jim said, picking up his controller and resuming the mashing of buttons, doing his best at indifference. He was a little buzzed from the beers, so as Jennifer's hand began to knead his thigh, he sighed.

"Maybe not all the trouble," Jennifer said, leaning toward him. She took the controller out of his hands and brought her face next to his. Poor woman was probably hard up for real affection. Jim's dad must have penciled in romantic interludes like they were rowing-machine workouts. Though he probably cuddled the rowing machine after.

Now Jennifer leaned over him so that her hair draped around his face. He hadn't been with a girl since he left boarding school, a fumbling good-bye with a classmate with whom he'd never made it official. ("Not official" was kind of his default.)

She smelled good, and as her hair brushed his cheek, Jim's mind went immediately to Juliet in the hallway that morning, the way she'd pulled a strand of hair around her finger and looked so doubtful about Romeo. Why were the girls who had the least to doubt always the ones who did?

And why was he thinking about Juliet when his dad's employee was about to kiss him?

He scrambled away from her on the couch.

"What the hell? What are you doing?" he said, noticing that Jennifer had already regained her poise and was looking at him with no real emotion in her eyes. He might as well have been some course-of-business thing, like a nondisclosure agreement or something.

"Good job, Jim," she said. "That was a test. You passed. I'll let your dad know."

As she clipped out of the room, Jim was starting to wonder if his loyalties were with the wrong person.

CHAPTER 10

JULIET

"MON ONCLE!" WHAT was it about her cousin Thibeau Capulet's voice that made it carry into every nook and cranny of the large Capulet mansion as if it owned the place?

Juliet was at her vanity, idly brushing her hair and staring at the row of perfume bottles but not really looking at any of them. The week's events had become a muddled mélange of scenes, from the hotel with Romeo, to the escape with Jim, the gala, school. Pierre had texted her sweet words all week—*Miss you, darling* and *Can't wait to see you again, my dear,* like they were ancient people who'd met on a cruise ship—but it had been Romeo's email to their secret account that she'd read again and again.

If you don't know that it's you, that it will always be you and has always been you, you should know. You are who I yearn for, no other, forever. . . .

God, she loved him.

But now here was Thibeau loudly sucking up downstairs to spoil her reverie. Juliet moved to the doorway of her room to hear what he was saying.

"Are we ready for the big day?" Thibeau was asking Maurice. As though he were really part of the "we." He wanted to be. And technically, he was next in line for the company after Henri. But he was undeserving and a slime. Plus, he was a high-stakes gambler, and Juliet suspected he was the one who had led Henri down the road to the money troubles that had forced Henri to sell those designs.

Juliet scowled and backed into her room to finish getting ready. Behind her, Lu Hai paused in folding Juliet's underthings to make a similar face that Juliet could see reflected in her vanity mirror.

"Someone forgot we take the trash *out* on Thursdays, not bring it back in," Lu Hai muttered nastily. She made no secret of her dislike of Thibeau. "I've smelled better things on Bourbon Street day after Mardi Gras."

Juliet giggled. Lu Hai's meaner pronouncements were, as Gabrielle would say, quite gangsta. And that was even more comical given Lu Hai's ancientness. She had to be a thousand years old.

"Did I say that out loud?" Lui Hai smoothed a wrinkle from an ivory camisole Juliet had last worn in bed with Romeo. "Oops."

It was a bigger morning than the start of Fashion Week. It was the day of the annual shareholders' meeting for the House of

Capulet. And, as a matter of fact, for the House of Montague, as well. This year, the stakes were even higher following the Redmond announcement.

In the early years after going public, the two houses had held meetings on separate days, until the heads of both learned that whoever went second had the upper hand. So now, each company had entire fall internships devoted almost solely to finding out when the other house was holding its meeting, with each house vying to ensure its announcement was later—and more high pro-file (and yet, somehow, more understated)—than the rival's. The spring event, because it followed Fashion Week, was always pivotal, as both houses reinforced the strength of their fall lines and campaigns.

Juliet would be playing her customary role of interested and dutiful daughter, and sitting, as usual, in the front row, next to Thibeau.

Not too far away, Romeo would be in the same role—but of dutiful son—for the House of Montague meeting.

For now, Henri would be on stage, standing beside their father like the next in line the public believed he was. The Capulets had a long history of admiring females as objects of beauty only. Progressive notions of putting a woman at the helm had never infected the Capulet line.

But this week her father had actually engaged her in passing for brief tête-à-têtes about some bit of news from the design team or the marketing people. He'd always relied on Juliet for the "girly details," as he called them, but the questions he was asking her—would it be a coup to source some fabric from female entre-preneurs in the third world (not just a coup, the right thing to do, Juliet had said), for example—were bigger than just, were the cloth buttons for the new Antigone topcoat more interesting cov-ered in leather or lace? (Lace over leather, Juliet had urged.)

But any real change in his attitude was probably only in her imagination. After all, it was the morning of a big event and Juliet had done nothing but get groomed. She'd rather have been in school than made to be another well-dressed prop. Still, as she slid into the House of Capulet's spring triumph, the Peony Dress, she allowed herself a few moments of pleasure.

New clothes really did feel exquisite.

Fitted like a forgiving, ethereal ballet dancer's tutu, the Peony Dress was already the star of the spring lines. Not just the Capulet spring lines, but *all* the spring lines. No fashion house anywhere—Paris, Milan, New York—had so captured the public's imagination with something fresh the way this dress did. It was part of a story, as Juliet had told her father. "You can't just expect a dress to sell, Papa," she'd told Maurice. "It has to be part of a fantasy."

So when the dress debuted, it was part of an entire mid-summer's night landscape—models dressed as fairies and fawns and flowers, with Tamar Descartes, a previously unknown model, wearing the dress and posing in the center of it all. Tamar was now, mere months later, a household name. And the dress was already the most copied design of the Fashion Week shows, and had ushered in a "new era of magic," according to *Maintenant.*

Juliet hadn't really thought it was such a big deal—didn't the designers and marketers know by now that every young woman wanted to feel swept into a fairy tale but still hold the reins of her destiny?

Now, Juliet's phone buzzed. It was her mother calling from the parlor. "Juliet," Hélène said into the phone, urgency in her voice. "Are you ready?" Juliet cringed. No doubt Maman would want to see to it that her lipstick was perfect, her hair properly chignoned. Juliet was fairly certain her mother hadn't picked up a book in years, unless you counted the September edition of *Vogue*. She sometimes said that thinking too much gave a woman wrinkles. Juliet knew her mother was no idiot, though. Hélène just preferred to avoid facing difficult things.

"Yes, Maman," Juliet said. "All dressed."

"Good, your father is on his way up," Hélène said.

Interesting. Maurice must have really been panicked to come to Juliet's room with a query. Usually, he fired questions at her over breakfast or in the back of their chaffeured Mercedes. Always in passing, probably so she didn't get any ideas that she was too valuable a consultant.

A few short raps came at the door and Lu Hai went to answer it, standing behind the door as she swung it open. Maurice sidled into the room, his footfalls heavy on the dark hardwood. The rest of Juliet's room was done in varying shades of white and pale pink. The four-poster bed was covered with a sumptuous ivory goose-down bedspread and hung with sheer rose-tinted drapes. A white and gold-thread rug handmade in Marrakech unfurled beneath the bed. A low chaise in cream lolled dreamily under a huge picture window that looked out over the fashionable street below and all of Paris beyond. Next to the bed were stacks of the old books and fashion magazines Juliet liked to buy at flea markets, and scattered around were small knickknacks that had caught her eye in vintage stores: carved wooden peacocks, small jewelry boxes inlaid with colorful tiles, old postcards in gold frames. Her favorite part of the room, though, was a small balcony that overlooked the yard and private street next to the Capulet manse. She'd told Romeo about it, teasing that he should come shout for her from below. Sometimes at night, if she heard a noise from the flower beds, she'd imagine Romeo was there. Of course, he never was.

Juliet looked around her room, somehow self-conscious to have her father here. But Maurice took no notice of anything as he folded his large frame into a delicate birch-wood chair.

"What is it, Papa?" Juliet asked, turning from her vanity to regard her father. Maurice was broad-shouldered and jowly and never looked happy.

"It's about the meeting today," he said, looking around the room like he expected to see an intruder.

When his eyes landed on Lu Hai, the servant asked, "Shall I go?"

He waved a hand at her. "No, you are loyal. You can stay."

Maurice looked at Juliet now. Really looked at her. Could he see her thoughts? Did he know the truth about Romeo? Juliet's heart raced. Though they often talked, this was especially careful attention on her father's part and she wasn't sure she liked it.

"Henri is no longer fit to lead, as you know," he said. Now, he looked at his hands, as though asking them why his only son had to disappoint him the way he did. "But I don't like Thibeau. He is strong, and he will do fine. I just don't like him."

Juliet laughed.

"We agree on that, I know," Maurice said. "I need a youthful face to present today, to remind the public that we have more to us than an old man like me. Especially at a time like this. In fashion, someone my age might as well be dead."

"Don't say such things, Papa," Juliet said, now getting up to put a hand on her father's shoulder.

He shook his head. "It is life, to die. That's not the point here," he said. He looked up at her. "It's a different thing altogether to let yourself be killed. I need you to deliver a speech this morning, something to please the investors, show them we are still full of youth and beauty. That this American and his pledge to do us in is nothing more than a wrinkle to be ironed out."

Juliet felt weak. This was too much. Too much for a sixteen-year-old who only wanted to be with her boyfriend. Just days ago she'd been hoping to run away, and now here was her father, doing what? Was he asking her to play a bigger role with the company?

"But, Papa," she said, "they won't take me seriously."

Maurice smiled. "You'll be fine," he said. "I'm not giving you the keys. Just a speech, marketing approved. I haven't read it." He handed her some notecards. "Do you prefer I email it or text it or whatever you do?"

"This is fine," Juliet said, scanning the cards as her stomach flipped over. She shook her head. "But I'll be in front of all the shareholders."

Maurice shrugged. "You look beautiful. Isn't that all a woman needs to feel her best?"

Juliet rolled her eyes. It was a wonder her father could survive in the modern world with ideas like that. "Papa, I need much more than that."

He stood up. "Okay, I will ask Thibeau."

"*Non.*" Juliet reached for his arm. "I will do it."

Maurice grinned in a way that showed Juliet he'd had no intention of using Thibeau and that her cousin's name had been dropped solely to provoke her. "You do whatever it is you need to feel your best."

"But we leave in an hour!"

Maurice shrugged as he walked out the door. "Capulets learn quickly. And the speech is written. Now you just need to deliver it."

Juliet felt like this was large and important. What did it mean? Did she want what it meant?

She turned to Lu Hai, who was better to talk to about these things than her mother. "Do you think he wants to turn the company over to me?"

Lu Hai shook her head. Not in a "no" way but in a way that indicated Juliet had much to learn.

"He never said that," Lu Hai said. "A good rule in life is not to hear words that are not said."

CHAPTER 11

JULIET

THE CAPULET MEETING was to be held at the Musée Rodin, a small museum in the Seventh Arrondissement that was dedicated to the art of the famous sculptor. The works were housed in an eighteenth-century chateau with stunning grounds. For the shareholders' meeting, the entire interior had been filled with both real and silk flowers, mostly peonies, for an explosion of color and fragrance. The effect was opulent without being circus-like.

Her father delivered the numbers portion of the presentation. Maurice was quite good at this. He was jocular when it came to discussing money.

"There's recently been gossip about our company being

purchased by an American. This James Redmond," he said. His face had grown a bit red, like just mentioning the name "Redmond" was enough to cause him anger. "But I want you all to know that our company is vital, and too important to France to let it fall into the wrong hands. The idea that we'd merge with our longtime competitors, the House of Montague, is even more ludicrous. . . ."

He was certainly mincing no words. Next to him, Henri stood bolt upright, as if to demonstrate that the company was strong.

In the echoey museum, Juliet could hear the scribbles and taps of journalists writing and typing their stories as Maurice spoke. The meeting was bigger news than usual, no doubt due to Redmond.

"And now, I'd like to conclude by introducing you to a face you all know and a mind you've not yet had the chance to meet. My daughter, Juliet, is my secret weapon in figuring out what our youth will wear. And certainly hearing from someone more fashionable than I am should inject faith in you all for our coming success."

It was quite an introduction, though after Lu Hai's words, Juliet noticed that he didn't say she was his successor. As she stood up to take her father's place on the makeshift stage, Juliet realized that she'd never paid much attention at these meetings before. And she'd always been in the front row. So as she got behind the podium, she saw just how many people filled the room. And just how many people were looking at her expectantly. She'd delivered speeches with aplomb at school. Juliet had a natural ease at speaking because she was wise enough to know that it was one of those things that was not a matter of life and death, and too many people treated it that way.

But before, the words she spoke had been *hers*. She glanced down at the cards her father had given her. Her speech, which she'd begun to memorize in the car, looked like nonsense to her. She closed her eyes and let the sentences come into focus. Words like *youth, glamour,* and *spirit* sprang out at her. And to Juliet they seemed like a jumble of, well, bullshit. So she set the cards on the podium and said what she knew to be true.

"I am Juliet Capulet," she started. "I am sixteen. I go to school, I see my friends, I think about the future, I think about who I want to be. I sometimes have crushes. I dream of falling in love."

Here, she looked down at her father and mother. They smiled benignly at her, like this was a school play, and she guessed that neither of them were aware she wasn't reading from the cards. They'd never expect her to go off-book. Henri, however, who'd taken his seat in the audience as well, must have known right away that she was making it up as she went. Her brother smiled, almost gleefully, and made a silent clapping gesture with his hands. Next to him, Thibeau looked smug, as though Juliet were failing and he believed himself to look the better for it.

"Well, today we are here, in the Rodin Museum, and there are two sculptures here that speak to me," Juliet said. She felt like she was at confession, because everything she was saying was true. "There's *The Thinker,* maybe Rodin's most famous work, and *The Kiss,* which has been copied in fifty percent of perfume advertisements for the last one hundred years."

Here, the crowd laughed. Juliet was surprised how satisfying it was to have gotten it out of them.

"But the point of them is, to me, the head and the heart. We are all ruled so very much by our heads, and what we know we should do and how we know we should act, and what we know to be best for us. Or what we think we know."

One of the publicity team members had scurried to the front row and was whispering something in Maurice's ear. Likely something about how the speech Juliet was giving was not the speech she was supposed to be giving.

Her father glanced up at her, and while he didn't look happy, he didn't look mad, either. The familiar furrow between his brows appeared as he frowned.

"But then you see something like *The Kiss* and you realize that, well, if we are just thinking all of the time, we will all be sitting alone. We need to be ruled by the heart, too. The thing that drives us to kiss, and to fall in love . . ."

From the far back of the room, a skinny man had stepped into the aisle. He had on a pair of cropped black pants, held up by red suspenders that matched his patent loafers. He clutched a notebook and was obviously a reporter of some kind. "Are you in love with someone, Juliet?" he asked.

Juliet felt color flood her face and knew it was probably apparent even from the back of the room. "I could be, but it's no matter," she said. She smiled sweetly at him. "And certainly not important to the shareholders." Even if it was. The news of Juliet and

Romeo—the enemy houses tied through young romance—would be a scandal for the ages.

"Well, is there a point to this?" the man asked in a snide tone.

"Yes," she said, urging strength into her voice. "Yes. It is that we are a company that knows the smart thing to do is to be in the hearts of our buyers. There is no loyalty without love. And as we face these new challenges, and fight off this new threat of James Redmond, we will win no battles without a brand about which we are passionate. We need all of you to fall in love again—and stay in love—with Capulet."

In the front row, her father looked stunned.

But also . . . proud.

And as the audience rose to its feet, Juliet was shocked to acknowledge that she felt the same way.

CHAPTER 12

ROMEO

"GO CHANGE," ROMEO'S father told him. "I don't want you wearing all black, like you're at the company's funeral."

Romeo looked down at his suit and tie. He liked wearing all black. He looked good in it. And besides, the suit was the same one that Cole Mohr was wearing in the House of Montague's spring campaign, and Romeo looked arguably better in it. There shouldn't have been an issue.

But ever since that James Redmond guy had popped up at the Palais party, Jean Montague had become a nasty stress case. Romeo knew it was a big deal. Even though his dad thought he wasn't paying attention, Romeo had heard enough about Redmond to know his buying the company and merging it with the House of Capulet wasn't exactly desirable. Far from desirable. Like the Capulets, the Montagues thought being lumped in with their archrivals just added insult to injury.

"Wear the navy, with a light blue shirt. Blue relaxes people." That Jean Montague was himself not at all relaxed in his blue shirt and navy suit was evidently lost on him as he advised his son.

"Dressing like a matching father-son set isn't really going to make us look strong, Dad," Romeo said, watching as his father scrolled through his phone for the fourth time in the last minute. He was waiting for the other shoe to drop, an expression that Romeo never understood but that seemed to apply here.

"Just change," Jean said, not looking up from his email.

Minutes later, they were in the back of the limo, which Romeo hated. Its heavy AC and darkness made him feel like a cloistered old man. When he was on a motorcycle or even in his Lambo, he felt like he was part of the rhythm of the city that he loved.

His mother was fawning over him, petting his hair like he was a child. Given that at least no one could see him in here, he let her. Catherine Montague had only had one child, Romeo, and she made Romeo acutely aware of that fact. Though she'd been a successful model and designer before meeting Jean, the company was old-fashioned enough that she wasn't expected to participate in the business side of things. After having Romeo, his mother had mostly retreated to a domestic role, as well as continuing to serve in that age-old female function: as the trophy wife. It was a shame because she was much more creative than his father, and capable of examining a problem from all sides.

They rolled through the streets of Paris, crossing the bridge over the Seine to go to the Île Saint-Louis, a small island in the middle of the river, often called the heart of the city. For the shareholders' meeting, the House of Montague had erected a tent on the street outside Berthillon, an ice cream shop known for its unusual flavors. Inside, models wearing pastel-colored jumpsuits from the Montague spring collection would be handing out cones in matching colors. The shareholders may not have been the most fun bunch on the planet, but they liked anything that made them seem like they were. Plus, the ice cream might detract from the fact that the House of Montague profits for the ending fiscal year were not what the company had projected. Normally, Romeo wouldn't have been apprised of this fact, but after the Redmond news, Romeo couldn't help but overhear his father's many tortured phone calls. Clearly, this wasn't going to be the best of meetings.

His father was still hunched over his phone when he let out a *"Zut alors"* under his breath.

"What is it?" Catherine asked him, finally letting her hand drop from Romeo's hair.

"This." Jean turned the phone so the screen was facing Romeo and his mother. On it, Juliet's lovely face stared back in a close-up from a video. She was standing behind a podium at the Musée Rodin, her cheeks flushed pink. Romeo had to keep himself from smiling. He'd been with a lot of gorgeous women, but Juliet's face was the first that could instantly bring a smile to his lips.

His father hit the *Play* arrow in the center of the screen and Juliet came to life. She was delivering a speech to the House of Capulet's shareholders, and she was, well, captivating.

At once self-possessed but modest-seeming, she positively glowed as she talked about the company's future. When they came to the end, Jean refreshed his screen.

"The commenters love her," he said, furiously tapping the screen. "And the business reporters can't stop talking about her. She goes to your school, doesn't she? Of course, you wouldn't associate with Capulet trash."

Now Jean was looking across the seats toward Romeo. He did know Juliet. And associated with her. Intimately. Even though he knew his father had dismissed the idea of him ever talking to her—a positive of all Romeo's previous conquests was Jean's notion that, with so many other options, Romeo would certainly overlook Juliet—he felt for a second like his dad could read his mind, and he felt protective toward his private thoughts of Juliet.

"She's just another girl," Romeo said with a shrug. It was the understatement to make all other understatements sound like exaggerations.

"Clever of Capulet to have her give the speech," Catherine piped up. "She's very pretty and self-possessed. Modern."

"Yes, she's very good at this," Jean said, shooting Catherine a dirty look as if she should know better than to say anything flattering about his rival. "Leave it to that slob Maurice Capulet to whore out his daughter like that. The son is probably too stupid."

Romeo didn't know whether he should feel proud that Juliet had impressed his father so, or angry that Maurice Capulet had used her, as Jean suggested. "Let me see it again," he said, reaching for the phone.

Jean handed him the phone with a bemused look. "I never knew you cared about our competition."

Ha, if we can just keep you from knowing, Romeo thought.

He pressed *Play* to start the video. An affectionate smile started to pull at his lips as Juliet stepped to the podium. Romeo knew her well enough to discern a nervous quaver in her "Hello," though her voice came through quite strong. Even though she'd seemed quite self-assured their first time together—she knew what she wanted, always—he remembered a tiny tremor in her voice and the tiny goose bumps on her slender arms as they'd made their way to the bed.

As she continued to speak, her confidence rose. Her cheeks were flushed but not in a way that suggested anything more than warm lights and enthusiasm. She had a magnetism that came through even on the tiny screen. She radiated love and warmth, and Romeo felt almost jealous of the audience, like they were enjoying the comfort of her that he wanted to belong only to him.

What a fool he'd been, to have not stolen more time with her at the gala, or not to have seen her since then. He hoped she knew that his evening with Rosaline had been nothing.

"What do you think?" Jean asked Romeo. "We should have thought about this. The Capulets are assuring their people that the future is in their hands, and we're handing out ice cream cones."

Romeo wondered suddenly about his father's business acumen. It was smart for the Capulets to show their company was in good, young hands—though Juliet had never mentioned to him that the business would be hers or that she had any role in it whatsoever.

He also wondered why his father hadn't thought to use him the same way Maurice Capulet had used Juliet. Was Romeo not strong enough? Not smart enough to stand up and speak to the board? Juliet was a better student than he was, and he would have trusted her to run a company. God, maybe he *should* have run away with her to start their own business.

"I think she's pretty great," Romeo said. Again, it was an understatement, but at least it came closer to the truth.

His mother squeezed his arm. "You would do even better," she said. "It's too bad that now it would look like we were copying them."

But Romeo didn't know about that. Juliet would have been impressive even if he didn't love her. How had he never paid more attention to this side of her before, realized her full power?

He was stupid—an ignorant male. He knew her, he pretended to know her, but there was so much more to know. Just because you'd found your one, felt known and like you knew, it didn't mean that you really knew everything. Just that you could keep learning about them and only grow more amazed.

His sudden awareness of all that was left to know of her assured him of another thing: He needed to see her. Now. Or as soon as humanly possible.

Handing the phone back to his father, Romeo pulled out his own phone and started an email to the secret account. *Let's meet,* he wrote. *Somewhere different this time. Special. Details soon. I love you.*

CHAPTER 13

JULIET

SHE'D BEEN ON the verge of fresh ire toward Romeo when his message had come, saying he needed to see her. Days had passed since she'd heard from him—that message from him that she was his only one. It had been almost a week since the gala and Rosaline. There should have been more. A rendezvous, even a reckless, short one, to prove he meant what he wrote.

Then, school and the meetings. Since the Capulet one yesterday, Juliet felt flush with her success, and she wished she could share it with Romeo.

Now, maybe she could, but she wanted something more from him. That he needed to see her, fine, it would be a lie to say that she was not excited at the prospect, even if she thought it should have happened sooner. But where, at least, was the groveling? The effects of his earlier message were still there, but that it had taken him so long to write more had left her hoping for a better invitation. After Rosaline, she merited better prose than "Let's meet." They might as well have been a study group.

Even as she rode the high of her presentation to the shareholders, Juliet's anger was still piqued at the whole Romeo and Rosaline thing, and it was made worse by the fact that she couldn't even ask him what had gone on. To be a girlfriend who had no access to her lover was starting to make her wonder if they really had anything together. Did he really mean that "now and forever" stuff or was it just a way to keep her around? Did he love her for the secret, or because it was real?

She told herself it was the latter. To be held by Romeo was all the proof of his love she required. It sounded silly, but they didn't have a connection—they were *connected*. Her soul found purchase on his. He was her safe place, even though he made her feel miles above the ground.

But when would Romeo be brave enough to step forward and say they were together?

Since the gala, Juliet had wanted to say something. Not just because of Rosaline but because, well, what were they hiding for? She knew. She did. She looked around her room, filled as it was not only with comforts but with tokens and memories of her very comfortable life. On her bookcase were the old editions of fairy-tale books she used to collect, her father bringing her back a different version from every city he visited. On her vanity were silver-framed photographs of her and her parents skiing in the French Alps and aboard the Capulet yacht. Tucked into the corner of her mirror was a strip of photos of her and Henri, curling at the edges. They'd taken them at an arcade in London, where they'd gone on a whim when Henri graduated from high school.

She didn't want to be disowned. But she had to wonder, would her family really disown her over a boy? True love seemed like it should be harmless. But her father's words always echoed: "Juliet will do what's good for the company."

She was the apple of her father's eye and she enjoyed her hold on his heart, but did it mean that she would always have to rein herself in?

Surely, love couldn't mean only doing what would rock no boats, cause no harm, make a person feel smaller, rather than bigger.

It should have made a person courageous and brave. Maybe it was time to ask him point-blank: Was Romeo keeping her at bay just so he could meet her in hotel rooms while he took models to fancy parties? Or was he too scared to really risk anything for her? Both options galled her.

Feeling a bit high on her own capabilities, she decided she would tell him, today. Facing herself in the tall gilt mirror that stood beside the expansive picture window, Juliet wove her long tresses into an almost-severe bun at the back of her head. She wanted to look not like a girl in love but a woman with a plan. She tucked a plain white blouse into a pair of slouchy trousers— they were men's pants that she'd found at a thrift store and had sized for her body. The look reminded her of a picture of Bianca Jagger—a former Face of Capulet—that hung in her father's office. Juliet leveled a glance at herself in the mirror, pretending she could see Romeo across from her, practicing how not to care. Not caring was never easy when you had to try.

"Are you going to be the boss, little girl?" Lu Hai said with a touch of amusement.

Juliet started. Her nanny could sometimes be so silent, Juliet forgot she was there.

"No," Juliet said. "I just need to take care of some business."

"Well, that's how you get to be the boss," her nanny said, going back to her tidying. If Juliet ever did rise to the helm of Capulet, Lu Hai would be one of her deputies.

A light knock came at the door. Its irritating cadence could only mean it was Hélène. Juliet supposed she should be grateful for the warning knock, at least.

Lu Hai swung open the door, not bothering with a greeting. Even though Hélène didn't really want to raise Juliet herself, she had always treated Juliet's nanny as an intruder. But then, Hélène treated the entire household staff with a polite distrust.

"You're wearing a lot of makeup" were the first words out of Hélène's mouth on seeing her daughter. Really, Juliet wasn't wearing much at all—though she had taken extra time this morning, because even with her anger at Romeo, a part of her felt guilty, too: She'd woken up from yet another dream about Jim that made her blush just to think of it. It was the manifestation of her anger at Romeo, she'd reassured herself, not really believing it.

"It's not much," Juliet said. Thinking of Jim and Romeo, she couldn't meet her mother's eyes.

"It looks heavy," Hélène said. "But maybe that's just your face."

Her mother's nasty comments toward her came whenever Hélène herself was feeling less than her best. And indeed, Hélène looked drawn and tired. She wore worries the way other women wore oversized earrings. Juliet would have asked her mom what was wrong but knew better. Nothing upset Hélène more than knowing someone knew she was upset.

"I'm meeting Gabrielle," Juliet lied, mentally pulling together what Metro lines she'd need to take to get to the apartment building in the Eighteenth Arrondissement. She'd been surprised Romeo had wanted to meet somewhere as fashionable and tourist-friendly as the village of Montmartre, but the apartment, he'd said, was empty, the couple he'd rented it from having just left on a monthlong trip to South America. Juliet had looked up the ads for the spot herself, and there was something almost grown-up to her about staying in a home instead of a hotel.

"Oh, Gabrielle," Hélène said. "She'll surely be wearing more makeup than you."

"That girl's more overdone than a Mardi Gras float," said Lu Hai, who hadn't liked Gabrielle since the model had literally looked down at her and said, "I had no idea they made people so short."

"Have you heard from Pierre?" Hélène asked with less interest than was typical for her nosier questions. When her mother was in particularly irritating form about Juliet's lack of a boyfriend, her questions practically reached inside Juliet's brain to rifle around for the truth.

"A few messages since the gala," Juliet said. She wasn't lying. In the days since the gala, he'd checked in on her and even sent her a link to a slideshow of images from the gala where their photo was featured. They were standing with half a foot of space between them. Two slides later were Romeo and Rosaline, the model pressed close to Romeo's side. "He's very sweet." Another truth. She couldn't fault Pierre for trying.

"Sweet," Hélène tutted. "The poor boy should know you'd like him better if he were less sweet. Probably if you couldn't have him, you'd be in true love."

Juliet rankled at the comment, because it struck so close to part of her truth. She opened her mouth to protest but Hélène was already moving about the room nervously, stopping to look at the photos of Henri and Juliet.

"Have you heard from Henri?" She looked right at Juliet like she expected Henri to be hiding behind her back.

"I haven't seen him since the shareholders' meeting," Juliet said. Henri had excused himself from the postmortem by saying he had to meet a friend. There'd been a moment of awkwardness between them. Juliet felt strange that she'd done so well at her speech and enjoyed it so much. And she'd never even asked Henri how he felt about it.

But the advantage to Henri was that the excitement over Juliet's success yesterday had allowed him to escape without a lot of questions. Usually his abrupt vanishings set both parents on edge, given his past, but they'd been so focused on the positive press following the meeting, they'd been fine letting him go.

"Well, he didn't make his appointment yesterday," Hélène said. "And he's not answering his phone. When you see Gabrielle, check with her, please."

Henri's appointments were his Narcotics Anonymous meetings. They weren't as anonymous as they were for other people, since the House of Capulet sent a representative to ensure Henri made it inside the building. Gabrielle ran in some of the same party circles Juliet's brother used to frequent, with models and socialites, and occasionally Henri tried to have a social life. Thus Hélène's belief that the model might know her son's whereabouts.

"I will," Juliet lied, suddenly anxious to get out of this house and to the Montmartre apartment.

"I know," Hélène said, patting Juliet tentatively on the shoulder, like it was a trick she'd learned in Mothering School that she hadn't quite mastered. "Because you are our good little girl."

Juliet, "good little girl" that she was, didn't disagree.

She decided to take the car and driver part of the way to Montmartre, getting out near the Pompidou, where she'd claimed she was meeting Gabrielle. Then she could ride the Metro the rest of the way to Romeo.

She was nervous and jittery about what she would say. She'd read in some dumb magazine of her mother's that you should visualize what you wanted the outcome of a thing to be and you might get your desire. But she could only see as far as the argument: Romeo protesting, taking her in his arms, kissing her. The world around them slipping away.

But if she always let the world slip away when she was with him, how would they ever be a part of it?

Still, when she tried to imagine their big reveal—what, would Romeo trot her out in front of his parents at a family dinner? Would she bring his mother a hostess gift? *Here are some Ladurée macarons to make up for years of our families hating one another?*

Why did that seem remotely possible? It was, in some way, what she wished could happen. If she could just get past Romeo's passionate embrace and reassurances that he loved her and no other, maybe she could make it so.

Or maybe the kisses and reassurances would have to be enough.

Her driver stopped in front of the Pompidou, and Juliet sprang from the car, eager now to get to her train.

The museum plaza was swarming with people, many of them funneling into the building through the almost-exotic set of tubes that contained escalators zigzagging up the sides of the structure. If they were a normal couple, Romeo and Juliet would probably come here like other kids their age, posing for selfies as they rode up, Romeo's arms wrapped around her shoulders possessively.

Maybe someday, Juliet thought, running toward her Metro stop. She checked her phone quickly before descending the stairs. There was a message waiting.

A text from Gabrielle.

Need you to come now. It's Henri.

She gave an address in the Ninth. It was a financial district but it had pockets that were residential, and not all of them great.

It was not like Gabby to text with no joke, no smiley face, no friendly dig at Juliet's supposedly good-girl life. And it was about Henri. If he'd been missing and he was with Gabrielle, it might mean he hadn't been able to resist the temptations of an unhealthy crowd.

Juliet navigated to the secret account and wrote a short message to Romeo: *Something's come up. Something important. I can't make it. I'm so sorry, my love.*

Reluctantly, regretfully, she left it in the drafts folder, as they always did, hoping he would know to check it.

Because she wasn't meeting Romeo any longer, and because she felt the urgency in Gabrielle's message, Juliet hailed a cab and asked it to take her as far as the Printemps department store. She would walk the rest of the way. It wasn't far, and if the cabbie recognized her, she couldn't risk him being the type to supplement his income by selling a story about Juliet's mysterious stop.

When she arrived, sweaty in her long sleeves, she double-checked the address on her phone. The gray building was somewhat nondescript, especially for Paris. Its utter plainness made it stand out.

It was a corporate housing apartment that seemed designed precisely so no one would want to stay too long. The lobby was as drab as the exterior, as if to remind residents that they were just here to work and nothing more.

Juliet signed in as Beatrice Rien (French for "nothing") with the indifferent guard, purposely writing in an illegible scrawl when she added the apartment number she was visiting. She took the elevator to the ninth floor.

The door to 907 was partially open and she pushed in. The apartment wasn't large, but the lack of much furniture made the space look bigger. A party had obviously been held here recently. The room was strewn with half-empty beer bottles, glasses containing dregs of dark red wine, liquor bottles lying on their sides. Stale smoke hung in the air, making the room taste like what gray looked like. Someone had been sick in the middle of the action. Or so suggested the noxious odor that saturated the air.

But there were only two guests left. Gabrielle was on the couch, cradling Henri's head in her lap. Juliet rushed to them, knocking her knee into a coffee table and toppling several bottles.

"What happened?" she demanded. Her brother's face was wan as he looked up helplessly into hers. His green eyes lacked all of their usual movement.

"Some of us went to a club—well, a warehouse thing really." Gabrielle's voice shook. "Henri was there with me and some of my friends. It was fine," she said, trailing off. She looked for a long time at Henri's face, like she hoped to revive him with her gaze. "We were just dancing. Mostly. Henri was just dancing."

Juliet knew that if Henri wanted to stay off drugs, he needed to stay away from where they were. There was no such thing as "just dancing" to Henri.

"This guy took me aside," Henri said, wobbling over the words. "And he had . . . stuff. It was like he knew everything about me. Or at least who I can turn into."

A sudden shiver took hold of Henri and his body quaked.

"Whose apartment is this?" Juliet asked. "How did you wind up here?"

Gabrielle shook her head. "It was the same group. Henri thought it would be a good idea to go lie down somewhere anonymous until things wore off. But then there was more. We fell asleep here." Gabrielle looked at the couch, as if making sure it was indeed where she'd fallen asleep. "And when we woke, everyone was gone."

Henri spasmed, his body not his own. Juliet became even more certain this day wasn't going to end with her seeing Romeo after all.

"We need to get him home," she told Gabrielle. "Cleaned up first, though." Henri's clothes were stained with spills of other people's drinks, and he smelled like an ashtray.

"And then what?" Henri asked weakly. "I pretend I didn't use again and it just goes away?" His voice had a nastiness but Juliet didn't let herself take it personally.

"Yes." Juliet nodded, helping her brother to his feet. He was of slender build but right now felt like a ton of bricks the way his dead weight leaned against her. "We go home, we tell Maman that you met a girl and stayed out too late. Just shake your head if she asks about her. If she thinks you don't like her, she won't care."

"Wow, I'm glad I'm not dating one of you," Gabrielle said, but with a wistful look at Henri.

Juliet shushed her. Turning to Henri, she said, "You don't want to be exiled, so you will let me take care of you. Maman and Papa won't be the wiser if you just stay a bit hidden."

Henri's nod wasn't just one of bland acceptance. He respected what she was saying. Juliet felt again like she had after the speech, like she was a woman at the helm of some kind of destiny.

"And we'll find who did this," Juliet added now, perhaps heady with power.

Henri shook his head. "I did this," he said. "I can't trust myself out in the world."

As Henri moaned and turned onto his side, Gabrielle pulled Juliet into the kitchen of the dingy apartment. Juliet looked around. "Why are you the only two here?" she asked.

Gabrielle's glazed eyes surveyed the apartment, as though she was just really noticing that for herself. "Fashion people. They make a scene and they leave the mess behind as they skip to the next new thing." She looked impressed with her own observation. "Wow, I should be a writer when my breasts get saggy."

Juliet scowled at her friend. Now wasn't the time for The Gabrielle Show.

"I'm sorry," Gabrielle said, as if reading Juliet's mind. "I make jokes when I'm scared. I make a lot of them. I should probably look into that."

Then, snapping back to her original purpose, Gabrielle pulled Juliet into her. "Your brother, I think someone gave him something before he took anything," she whispered, watching to see if Henri was paying attention. "He was acting strangely. Loopy, out of sorts."

"Did you see anyone? Did you see who might have been near his drink, or who gave him the drugs?"

Gabrielle looked guilty.

"I was in no real shape myself," she said. "But every fashion house was there. It could have been anyone. I guess the question is, who'd most enjoy getting the best of Henri?"

The list, Juliet knew, was long, and included the name Montague.

CHAPTER 14

ROMEO

HE'D BEEN WAITING for an hour. Not even waiting. *Preparing.*

He'd bought food for an indoor picnic. Cheeses, bread, one of Juliet's favorite chocolate tarts. He had music playing. Wine chilling. Candles lit.

It was that standard kind of romantic in a way he knew Juliet didn't necessarily covet, but he'd wanted to do something for her in that cheesy lovestruck sort of way. These were the kinds of gestures he'd never made for his other girlfriends. No, not girlfriends. Trysts.

He wasn't sure how to show Juliet she was different. That he intended to be with her for a long time. Not a long time. Forever. He was only eighteen, but he'd lived enough to know that there was nothing he wanted more than her. That was part of the impetus for renting a real home for them and not just a hotel room. It seemed more grown-up, a way to say that someday they'd be the ones with the home.

And now came a cryptic message that she couldn't make it. What was "something important"? To him, there was nothing as important as being with her.

Walking through the apartment, he envisioned again how he'd planned to greet her, how he'd wanted to take her by the hand to the blanket he'd set up. He was going to pour her wine, serve her food, demonstrate in gestures what he never felt his words could say. Now that she wasn't coming, he felt like an idiot. Or like this was karma. Women had tried to prove they loved him with gestures that went beyond the bedroom, and he'd never really bitten. Was this the tables turning?

He held his phone in his palm, staring at the screen. He wrote back a simple message, *No problem. Hope things are okay.* Then he dialed Jim.

As soon as his new friend answered, Romeo asked him plaintively, "Have you ever boxed?"

A half hour later, Romeo was waiting at le Sports Club, a dingy gym in the Twentieth, a working-class arrondissement. He'd learned to box in the air-conditioned, fluffy-toweled confines of his father's gym, located in the very different Eighth. (The club catered to the very rich, and a single glass of Scotch cost as much as a yearlong gym membership somewhere else.) He'd trained with a former pro, who flattered Romeo and never swung too hard.

It was fine to learn in that gentle manner. But now, when he wanted to box, he came here, where the other clientele didn't care who he was and literally pulled no punches. Romeo was sweating as he pummeled a speed bag, waiting for Jim.

The distinctive roar of a Triumph tipped him off to his friend's arrival. How many bikes did this guy have?

Jim pulled open the smoked-glass door and looked around, evidently not expecting Romeo to have invited him to a place like this. It gave Romeo some satisfaction to not be exactly as Jim expected. It wasn't just bike-collecting Americans who had edge, he felt like saying. His need to impress Jim while also knocking him down a peg, he realized, was a sign that he genuinely wanted Jim's friendship.

Jim lifted a hand in that sort-of wave guys did that seemed to exist as a gesture only to prove to other guys that yes, you were here but no, you weren't all girly and excited about it. Romeo returned the gesture, his not-wave saying, *Yeah, you're here. Doesn't matter.* But he was glad to see Jim. And Jim had come a decent way to hang out on short notice. Responding to life—good and bad— like it didn't matter to you was a hard-and-fast rule of being a guy. It kind of stunk.

"Thought I had the wrong place," Jim said, pulling off his usual leather coat and tossing it haphazardly over the ropes. "You really work out here?"

Romeo shrugged, like he hadn't chosen this dingy place at least partially for its shock value. "A couple years now."

Just beyond the training ring was the weight-lifting and work-out area, where Romeo had been practicing the speed bag moments ago. He was glad to see the weights being used by Iago and Rolf, two regulars who were rumored to be members of rival street gangs. That he was here at the same time as potentially dangerous individuals had to show Jim he hadn't done the rich-boy thing of renting the place out (going the edgy-but-safe route).

He asked himself again, *Why do I care so much what Jim thinks?*

"So, you're probably a lot better than me, then," Jim said, actually sounding a little nervous. "Is there a reason our first hang is so you can kick my ass?"

Romeo hopped into the ring, feeling confident. "Let's box first, then talk."

"Opposite of how girls do it, isn't it?" Jim said, grinning.

The first time Romeo had hit anybody he'd been six years old, at a public garden with his nanny. A bigger kid had pushed him off a swing into some gravel. He'd swung and connected and it had felt good. Up until then, the only physical contact he'd ever had was affection: smothering hugs from his mother, doting caresses from his nanny, help with all his grooming and dressing from the Montague staff.

He got into fights sometimes, even now, but most guys at nightclubs didn't want to get into it too badly with a Montague. Partly because of his reputation and the entourage of guys who came everywhere with him and partly out of fear of the lawyers on retainer with one of Paris's oldest and most known families. (Not to mention whatever other sorts of wrath and ruin that family could rain upon someone who harmed them.) Even Benny hung back when they came here.

Jim, however, treated and punched Romeo like his equal. His first hit was square in Romeo's shoulder and sent him back toward the ropes. Then came another, from the other side, in quick succession.

Romeo bounced back to the balls of his feet, delivering a right hook to Jim's side. The guy was solid but the punch still sank deep—Romeo could feel it—and Jim stumbled back.

But he recovered his footing, his form solid, and parried back with a punch that Romeo caught with his glove.

It was the fairest of fights, and Romeo realized he was grateful for that day in Petite Asie, when he and Juliet had nearly been caught. He'd gained, somehow, a real friend out of it.

Jim knocked him back with a punch, forcing a burst of air from Romeo's lungs. The pain rang though him, but in the way he needed. He was sick of carrying around that hollow hurt in his chest, that wonder if Juliet was done with him. How perplexing that she could seem to want him so much but then just abandon him like that.

But his heart's ache was at least temporarily forgotten as he and Jim grappled. Every hit, bruising or not, felt good, pushing that empty feeling out of him.

It was something like love, when someone would hit you because you needed it.

They went on like this, throwing punches, hitting the ropes but not falling, until they were both sweating and panting.

Neither one was going to knock the other one out, so Romeo put his hands in front of him and said, "Let's take a break for that talk."

"Good idea," Jim said, and he didn't press the notion that they'd been having a match. He obviously didn't need to win. It showed he was as secure in himself as Romeo was.

In the back room of the boxing gym were a few card tables and folding chairs. Illegal card games went down here on the weekends and some nights. Romeo had played in a few. There was also Mathilde, a fifty-something woman with pillowy lips and breasts who poured her homemade whiskey into tumblers for members like Romeo and their guests.

She brought the drinks and offered Jim a smile that simmered with promise—Romeo had turned down her offers to "make a man of him," not only due to Juliet but also because he already considered himself one. Jim smiled back at her and gave her an appreciative glance, but he, too, didn't drool for her. Benny had, but that was Benny.

"It's Juliet," Romeo said as he swigged a burning sip of whiskey. He probably should have asked for water, but he was waiting for Jim to do it first.

"I would have guessed," Jim said, taking his first swallow of Mathilde's concoction. He didn't flinch, Romeo noted.

"How come? Because she's too good for me?"

Jim slugged back more whiskey. The guy could no doubt

hang. "Well, that," he said, but in a way that made it clear he was joking. "I don't know. I've never really been in love before, but I would think it's hard to love someone you can't really be with. Like, you want them all the way but it's not even an option."

Romeo swirled his own drink in his glass. This guy had just arrived at the core of Romeo's heart. "Yeah, and then you think you're going to be with them, and they bail on you."

Now Jim pulled a face, as if to say, *That's rough.* He signaled Mathilde.

She bounced over and leaned down on the table so both boys could see deep into the crevasse of her cleavage. *"De quoi as-tu besoin?"*

Jim took a final sip of his whiskey and Romeo feared he'd order more. But instead, he said, "Two waters. My liver just aged twenty years with that."

"Sweet boy," Mathilde said, with some disappointment, as she went to fetch the waters.

"So, you think I'm hopeless?" Knowing that Jim wasn't made of steel made Romeo feel somehow safer owning up to his pathetic broken heart.

Jim shook his head. "I'm sure you're not," he said. "Let me guess. Girls usually make things easy for you."

"Yeah, maybe too easy. How'd you guess?"

"I'm not exactly a stranger to it," Jim said with a smirk. "I'm not saying I'm much of a catch or anything, but I always feel like the less I care, the more they like me. It's sad, really."

"I can't not care about Juliet," Romeo said. "That would be like not breathing. Excuse the incredibly lame analogy."

Mathilde arrived with the waters and placed them in front of her charges. "There's nothing more beautiful than heartbroken boys," she said. Romeo and Jim squirmed at the odd compliment.

"What I'm trying to say, in my own equally lame way, is that I think you and Juliet are something special," Jim said. "Let me talk to her for you. After I kick your ass in the ring. I'm feeling a little too in touch with my soft side."

Romeo stood up. "Yeah, it would be great if you could talk to her for me." He punched his fist into his palm. "I'll try to leave your mouth so you can still form words."

CHAPTER 15

JULIET

WHAT WAS IT about something going dreadfully wrong that made her feel so close to her brother? Since his relapse, Henri had been counting on Juliet to keep him on the straight and narrow. Or at least the straight.

They'd spent the weekend in the family's screening room, watching old black-and-white movies projected across the whole of one large wall. The curtains were drawn and they were still in their pajamas on Sunday. Strewn on the floor around them were old magazines and several board games they'd played a lot as kids.

Lu Hai had been in a few times to tidy up, most of the time being as unobtrusive as possible. Juliet knew that Lu Hai was checking on Henri, but the nanny had the sense to let Juliet be the one in charge. Henri would bristle if he thought his latest woes would get back to his parents.

Right now, he was idly flipping through the Netflix menus, looking for something that featured his screen crush, Audrey Hepburn. His ex, Caroline, looked a great deal like Audrey, if Audrey had traded her cigarette pants and ballet flats for leather pants, oxblood lipstick, and tight white T-shirts.

"Sabrina, non," Henri said, scrolling through his choices. He looked the very picture of louche, his ash-blond hair just disarrayed enough to be fashionable, his chest bared beneath a loose gray robe worn over his charcoal-colored silk pajama pants. Even in duress, the corners of Henri's mouth edged up in a smirk. If she didn't know him so well, Juliet would have agreed he had a hard time taking anything seriously.

"Roman Holiday, I hate that ending. *Breakfast at Tiffany's?"* Henri exhaled a plume of smoke that danced over the paused black-and-white image of Givenchy-clad Audrey on the screen. The door at the far end of the room opened enough to let Lu Hai slide through, clutching what had to be their fifth delivery bag of sushi from Côté on Rue Marbeau. Their daurade sashimi was Henri's favorite and the ultra-thin pieces of tataki salmon made Juliet's mouth water. They'd each consumed one of everything on the menu by now. The copious servings of wasabi seemed to be helping Henri transfer the withdrawal pains to a more healthy form of suffering.

"More fish and no vegetables in sight," Lu Hai said, setting the containers of food on the low coffee table and clearing the old ones. She examined the bottles of Orangina as she tossed them into the plastic bag.

"There's edamame," Juliet said, flinging off her blanket and reaching for the container of spicy tuna rolls. "And fish is good for me. Brain food."

"Yes, and you have school tomorrow," Lu Hai said. She ventured a glance at Henri, who'd skipped over the classics to search Kristen Stewart movies. Juliet was hardly a fan but she'd allow it, given Henri's condition. "Are you going to be ready?"

Juliet knew that Lu Hai's question was code for, *Will Henri be ready?*

"*Oui*, Henri is going to help me and read my essay on Voltaire." If it weren't considered beneath their family to take such a job, teaching would have suited Henri, Juliet thought. He was a passionate reader and learner.

"Every man is guilty of all the good he did not do," Henri said, putting on some Japanese horror film that Juliet could tell she would hate.

"For now, we just need him not to be guilty of doing anything bad," Lu Hai whispered to Juliet. "Don't worry, I'll keep an eye on him."

Juliet squeezed her nanny's hand. "I know."

On Monday, Romeo's response was still bothering her. His response to her bailing had been that terse little email. *No problem. Hope things are okay.* Was he angry? Where was the *I love you*?

It troubled her. Why wasn't he more . . . distraught? There should have been a follow-up.

Someone like Catrine or Margaux would tell her that Romeo was just afraid of feeling too much. But Juliet always thought that was the mantra of girls who'd been dumped. He feels too much? What lies women could tell themselves.

Juliet didn't want to admit it to herself, because it felt petty and common, but she supposed she wanted a side effect of her no-show to be that Romeo worried. That he might make clear that Rosaline was nothing. (Though the flip side of her mind said that if he were to make a big deal of saying Rosaline meant nothing, then it perhaps meant more than Romeo's failing to mention her altogether.)

So today she was a little early for school. She'd go to her locker and take her time. She'd avoid Catrine and Margaux outside and just let herself wait. For what, she didn't know. It wasn't as though Romeo could walk right up to her at school without starting rumors.

But if she could catch his eye in the hall, she'd know whether he felt her absence—and the loss of time with her—as acutely as she did.

Sharing a gaze would not be the same as sharing a hotel room, but it would be something.

The problem was that, when she walked up to her locker, someone was standing near it.

His back was to her, and it wasn't Romeo. She'd recognize

Romeo's form anywhere. But, she surprised herself to note, she recognized this form instantly, too.

Jim. He wasn't wearing his leather jacket—it was warm today. Juliet herself had on a wispy babydoll dress over a pair of cognac-colored cowboy boots that were extremely well trod-upon. His shoulder blades pressed against the back of his faded black T-shirt, which looked like it had been washed so many times she would bet it felt like velvet by now. Juliet had a penchant for worn-in clothing. It became part of the wearer.

"Hi," she said, to his back. He hadn't heard her come up.

When he turned around with that sure American grin on his face, something sparkled beneath her breastbone. But she told herself it was just that flash of seeing something agreeable to the eye.

"Hi," he said to her, but then he looked away, to her hands turning the dial on her locker. As she opened it, she was relieved to have nothing too embarrassing in view. A class schedule taped to the door, a hairbrush with tangles of her hair in its bristles, a near-gone bottle of Juliet by Capulet perfume, a battered copy of a dog-eared romance novel she, Catrine, and Margaux had been passing around, making notes in the margins of the juicy pages.

The halls were filling up more now and there was that feeling of eyes upon them. The watchfulness of other teenagers had a weight to it that alerted you to its significance, the same way a coat draped over your shoulders told you it was winter. Only in this case the weight told you that everything you did could be multiplied by hundreds of voices, repeating and inter-preting it.

He still hadn't said anything beyond his greeting. "So," Juliet tried, "are you finding things okay here?"

Jim looked at her for a second, as if the "here" she asked him about was somehow on her face, instead of the school, or Paris in general.

"Oh . . . yeah. It's good. Great."

He smiled then, and it wasn't his cocky American smile but something softer. He looked down at his shoes as if he felt . . . shy?

"Actually, you and . . . our mutual friend . . . are the only people I know here so far." The bell for their first class chimed and Jim looked up toward the ceiling, as if something would be there to remind them to start walking. Their shoulders almost touching, Juliet and Jim made their way along the now-teeming hallway.

"Our mutual friend?" Juliet raised an eyebrow, catching Jim's eye in her peripheral vision. She knew Jim was talking about Romeo, but something in her wanted to hear his name, gain more information.

Now Jim grinned his usual grin. "You know, Benedict," he said. "It's why I'm here. He was . . . worried about you."

Something like relief flooded Juliet's insides but it was mixed with irritation. Was sending a messenger as concrete a gesture as Romeo could make when they were not alone?

"There's an issue. It's with my brother," Juliet said. She noticed other students' eyes quickly raking over her and Jim. Her friends, and many other girls at Lycée Louis-le-Grand, were already in agreement that Jim was the hottest thing to hit the school in a very long time. It bothered her a little, on Romeo's behalf, but she couldn't argue Jim's attractions.

Jim's forehead crinkled in a question. "Your brother? Did he . . . find out about you and . . . our mutual friend?"

Juliet shook her head. "No, no, nothing like that." They'd arrived at her classroom but Jim showed no indication that he cared about the class he had to get to. She wondered if it was an American thing or a Jim thing. Leaning closer to him, she whispered near his ear. "He's had some problems with drugs in the past. There was an . . . incident . . . a few days ago, but I'm helping him get better."

Jim's face fell. "And that's why you couldn't meet Romeo?"

Juliet put a finger to her lips to signal Jim to be quiet. Her and Romeo's coupledom getting out in the halls of this school would be as bad as a legitimate gossip columnist hearing about it.

"Yes. I wanted to be there more than anything," she whispered. "But my brother needed me." She looked around as she spoke. Her brother's travails were better not mentioned in these halls, too. A slipup would become something major to use against Henri and the House of Capulet.

"You're a good sister, then," Jim said, his eyes kind. "I mean, from what I can gather. I don't have any siblings."

"You'll tell him?" Juliet asked quietly, as students were starting to funnel into the door past them. She wasn't normally the girl to linger outside class with a boy.

"Tell who what?" Catrine's voice rang behind her. Juliet cringed. Catrine and Margaux were her friends, for all intents and purposes, but she didn't like them, not really. They were climbers and sycophants at best, and Juliet always felt they would sell her out in a second if it assured their own rise.

It was yet another reason she and Romeo understood each other so well. They both knew what it was like to grow up not trusting that anyone really liked *you* so much as what you could do for them. Romeo had his cousin Benny, though, who anyone could see would take a bullet for Romeo. Juliet often wished she had a loyal girlfriend. Gabrielle she thought she could trust (she was an in-demand supermodel and had too much pride to rely on favors from anyone) but Juliet had grown habituated against the secret-sharing that was a hallmark of female friendship.

Juliet caught her mouth from hanging open. Thinking fast, she said, "Tell his driver to arrange to bring him to the party this weekend. You'll come, *oui*?"

She put a hand on Jim's arm and urged him with her eyes to please understand what she was talking about.

"The party, yeah . . . wait, the address?" Jim got it instantly, which had the double effect of flooding Juliet with relief and of making her feel that Jim might be someone she could befriend.

"Here," Juliet said, scribbling down her address on a piece of paper peeking from her class binder. She tore off the corner and gave it to him. "Two o'clock. It's a birthday party for my cousin Thibeau. Don't bring a gift. He's awful."

Jim laughed at Juliet's wry delivery as Catrine absorbed the exchange with hunger. She was like a vulture in Dior eye shadow.

"I'll be there, too," Catrine said to Jim, putting her face right in front of him. "It's sure to be a good time."

Jim's flirtatious smile to Catrine wasn't lost on Juliet.

And neither was the fact that it bothered her.

Just a little.

CHAPTER 16

JIM

HE'D BEEN TO parties before.

And not just boarding school parties in someone's room with pilfered pills and illegally bought beer.

He'd been to big-deal parties, parties his dad hadn't wanted to take him to, parties where the chances were fifty-fifty that he'd either sit silently in a corner all night or go to bed with some undulating cougar who'd try to give him money on his way out of her single-occupancy honeymoon suite.

He knew instantly that the Capulet party was completely different. And he was way out of his comfort zone. Even though Juliet had invited him as a cover for their conversation, he'd taken

the event fairly seriously. He'd changed his outfit three times—
and he didn't even have that many clothes. She hadn't said anything about a dress code, so he hoped a button-down shirt with
rolled sleeves was formal enough.

At ten minutes after the 2:00 p.m. start time, he rang the door-
bell to the Capulets' brick mansion on the Avenue Montaigne. He
could hear music and laughter inside and noted the tastefully
rendered BON ANNIVERSAIRE banner over the door. He held a
bottle of Dom he'd taken from the fridge at home. He didn't expect
Juliet to be impressed by it, but he couldn't come empty-handed.
And he hadn't brought a gift for her cousin Thibeau, just as she'd
instructed.

A petite Asian woman answered and looked him up and
down. There are people in this world who you know on sight can
kick your ass. This woman was no doubt one of them. Something
in her flinty eyes told him to stand up straighter. So he did, and
held out his champagne-free hand for her to shake. She definitely
wasn't someone you greeted with the customary French double-
cheek kiss.

"Who are you?" The woman gestured toward him with her
chin, like he wasn't worth the effort to point at him.

"Jim Re—Gardner." He caught himself about to say his father's
last name and corrected it, but did he see a flash of suspicion in
the woman's eyes? "I'm a friend of Juliet's from school. She invited
me." He realized his hand was still extended toward her.

"Lu Hai." She didn't take him up on the handshake, just

pulled him inside. "A friend of Juliet's from before you were born, Mr. America."

They were in a huge entryway that sprawled out into two enormous rooms on either side of a circular staircase. The two rooms were like mini extensions of the Palace of Versailles. Matching chandeliers hung from the ceilings like upside-down crystal wedding cakes. The walls were coated in golden brocade wallpaper festooned with velvety silhouettes of birds and flowers. He almost wanted to run his hands over it. The marble floors were the color of a Tiffany box, and in the center of each were matching rugs that showed off clusters of flowers, threaded through with golden embroidery.

Compared to the modern loft he shared with his father, this place was like living in some kind of Marie Antoinette–style dream sequence. But not in an old-lady way. It was cool, like he'd entered some kind of magical fairy-tale world. It suited Juliet. . . .

Juliet, who was impossible to hide even in this sea of people. He noticed her shiny dark hair immediately, her head tucked near that of her friend. Was it Margaux? Or the other one. Catrine. Ugh. He wasn't sure who was who. He only knew that they wore the same perfume and had been vying for his attention ever since Juliet had extended the invitation.

Now Juliet looked up and spotted him. A smile lit her face and sent an electric charge from his brain to his stomach. But wasn't that just him being glad to see a familiar face?

"Jim," Juliet said, practically floating over to him. She looked like a punk-rock fairy amid this setting. Her long hair was loose and a little messy, spilling over a brown leather jacket worn atop a navy shirtdress cinched at the waist with a wide necktie. On her feet were a pair of deep-cherry combat boots. Woven through her tresses were leather strings with charms on the ends of each. Any girl who saw her would want to copy the look immediately, but no one could pull it off with Juliet's effortless ease.

By contrast, Margaux and Catrine—now he remembered: The brunette was Catrine, the redhead Margaux—looked like sugar-drenched desserts in pastel dresses that, while not ugly, lacked magic. They were following Juliet over, their eyes locked on Jim as if he was a quarry they'd been waiting to spot. While normally the attentions of two pretty girls at a party would have at least struck him as the beginning to a fun game, he really wasn't up for their attentions at the moment.

"Here, let me take you around," Juliet said, grabbing him by the arm and pulling him into the crowd. She lifted a finger over her head in some sort of silent signal to her friends to fall back, and they did.

Now she bent toward Jim. He could smell her light perfume—fresh and citrusy, not floral. In her melodic French-accented English, she said, "There's really not that many people worth meeting here, but you should talk to my girlfriends—in a little while. They've been panting about your arrival all morning and I can't bring up our mutual friend, Benedict, in front of them. Besides, it's better for you if they can't get to you right away. Believe me, absence makes the heart more eager, if not fonder."

Jim raised an eyebrow. "Are you speaking from experience?" Across the room, Catrine and Margaux stood in wait, flutes of pink champagne held aloft. When they saw him look their way, both girls offered the same beckoning smile, and yet he was happier here, talking to Juliet. About her boyfriend.

But that was why he was here, wasn't it? To help his good friend Romeo clear up whatever misunderstandings were ailing his relationship with Juliet.

Juliet looked around the room and spoke in a low tone as if afraid to be caught. "It would be much easier not to love him."

"I don't think he'd like that at all." Jim had to edge closer to Juliet as an older woman passed behind his back.

"Sometimes I'm not sure," Juliet said, and her eyes flashed with a question. She really wasn't sure. He couldn't believe it.

"Romeo loves you," Jim said, his voice low.

But Juliet's eyes widened like a cartoon's. "Don't say his name here! Someone might drop a chandelier on you for treachery."

She pulled him through the crowd, stopping to introduce him as her new friend from school to a few people—cousins, family friends, an aunt here, an uncle there. Her life was so full, Jim thought. He came from a world where a family gathering meant he and his father would be in the same room for several minutes.

"Ugh, there are so many of them, *non*?" Juliet rolled her eyes as she bid farewell to a sweet-seeming uncle who'd asked Jim a series of questions about what to pack for a wintertime trip to New York. "Is your family so, how do I say it . . . on top of you?"

Jim thought of Jennifer, his father's assistant, and her seductive overtures a few days before. That it was the closest he'd come to something resembling familial affection was entirely disturbing.

"Yeah," he lied to Juliet. "It's kind of nice to leave that all in the States. But your family seems nice."

While he knew a lot of their peers hated to deal with family obligations, he meant this. Her family did seem nice. To always come home for a beer that no one would even scold him for taking, to play video games without limit, to do whatever he wanted because he could be certain that no one much cared—well, it would be a dream come true for plenty of guys his age, but it got old fast. He wondered if he'd ever enjoy a relationship with his father so good that he could almost take it for granted, the way Juliet seemed to. If he delivered on the information his dad wanted, would something good come of it? He really hoped so, because it wasn't easy to feel like he was lying to Juliet's perfect face.

Juliet had brought him to a table with a big birthday cake covered in a fondant that seemed to match the wallpaper. Around it were platters of lobster tarts and speared vegetables, fancy cheeses and pieces of crusty bread. Platters of sushi lay on beds of ice, around a raised table where a sushi chef was creating rolls by request.

"I bet you want a hamburger," Juliet said, looking at Jim as he surveyed the food.

"I like sushi." He honestly hadn't had a lot of it, given that his many northeastern and English boarding schools were more likely to serve clam chowder and fish and chips when it came to seafood. Still, Juliet's satisfied smile as she plucked a piece of sashimi with chopsticks and ate it in one bite convinced him he would like it.

"I only eat fish—I mean, of the previously living creatures."

Jim laughed, thinking of the steak dinner that was his father's idea of family time. "My father would hate you."

"Oh, really, and why is that? Who is your father to judge me?"

They were treading in dangerous territory, Jim thought. One wrong word and why wouldn't a smart girl like Juliet put it together that James Redmond had strolled into town around the same time Jim Gardner and all his rich-kid vehicles had shown up at her high school? His body gave him signs that he wanted to tell her the truth—the tense pull in his stomach, the guilty sweat that sprang from his pores when he even mentioned his father. Really, besides financially, his dad had barely been part of his life. He honestly felt closer to Juliet than he did his father. Still, there was all that blood-was-thicker stuff to think about, and he grew woozy wondering how his father would act if Jim sold him out and blew the mission.

"Just your average American. A heartland kind of guy," said Jim, even though his father was from New Orleans and was of questionable heart.

"Well, he can have his heartland," Juliet said with a mischievous glimmer in her eye. She picked up another piece of sashimi and lowered it into her mouth. With her long hair spilling over her shoulders, she resembled a mermaid on land. "But bread, cheese, something from the sea—what more do I need?"

The way she said it, like an invitation, she could get the whole world to give up meat on the spot.

He heaped a plate with sushi rolls, then felt self-conscious, like the boorish American he probably was to these people.

Juliet didn't notice, or at least didn't comment. Even though he wanted her to. He liked her teasing. He made a show of dabbing his roll with wasabi. Maybe a little too much, as his eyes started to water on the first bite. He was trying to ingest it in as manly a way as possible when a guy with that floppy movie-star hair girls loved tapped Juliet on the shoulder.

"Juliet, who is your friend?"

Juliet swallowed a mouthful of sushi and held up a finger for Prince Charming to wait. Jim could tell just by the way the guy's eyes tracked Juliet's movements that he liked her as more than a friend. The question Jim needed to answer was whether Juliet liked this guy the same way.

Which he only needed to find out for Romeo. Of course for Romeo.

"Pierre!" she said, with genuine surprise. "I didn't know you were coming."

"Your mother invited me," he said. In that instant, Jim knew Prince Charming didn't have a chance with Juliet and probably had uttered the words guaranteed to end any possibility of a chance. *Your mother invited me* were the words of a guy with no game, except maybe Tiddlywinks.

"Oh, Maman, *bien sûr*," Juliet said, in a tone that threatened to turn to laughter. Now she grabbed Jim's arm like he was escorting her to a dance. To Pierre, she said, "Have you met my new friend Jim?"

The way she said "new friend" held all the assurances of someone who was more than a friend and Jim took the bait, for Pierre's benefit.

"Jim Gardner," he said, his "this is mine" voice sounding more like his father's than he was used to. He shook hands with the cartoonishly handsome Pierre, thinking he should tell Romeo to kick this guy's ass. It wasn't fair, though, since Romeo and Juliet weren't a public thing. And didn't Romeo have his pseudo-date— Rosaline—for media consumption?

Maybe Jim was lucky to be single.

"Pierre LeFevre," the guy said in a tone that dripped with entitlement. As if Jim had any notion of what a LeFevre was.

"Well, glad you two could meet," Juliet said, steering Jim— plate still in hand—away.

"Did I just help you shut that guy down?" Jim asked, looking over his shoulder at the stunned LeFevre.

"I've been ruder and he always comes back. But at least he'll leave me alone for now." Her face had an impish quality about it as she said this, and Jim relished even more his role as her co-conspirator. "You see, he'll go talk to Thibeau. Maybe he thinks it will get him points. Too bad he doesn't know I *hate* Thibeau."

But sure enough, the LeFevre dude was clinking champagne flutes and greeting a guy Jim assumed had to be Thibeau, who wore his hair slicked back like he was trying to look the part of a rich douchebag villain. Pierre and Thibeau together looked like the kind of guys who would accidentally kill a hooker and hide the body.

"I want you to meet my brother," Juliet now said, rolling her eyes as Thibeau let out a loud laugh, and dodging other guests. Her avoidance wasn't cold, though, just familiar. What would it have been like to grow up with a house full of people like this?

"Is that Thibeau?" Jim pointed to the douchey guy, who was now greeting guests like he owned the place. There was something nasty to his eyes, even when he smiled.

"Ew." Juliet practically spat. "Yes, that's Thibeau. The undeserving guest of honor I told you about. My cousin. Remember, we do not like Thibeau. Or I do not openly. The rest of the family pretends to."

Jim grinned. "You're so sweet and innocent seeming, and here you are breaking hearts and badmouthing family."

"I'm not sweet, nor innocent. And he's a jerk, believe me."

She squeezed his hand and pulled him around a table buried under a mound of gifts, presumably for the atrocious Thibeau. "My brother's name is Henri. He'll like you. You've probably been kicked out of some of the same boarding schools."

Jim laughed, and felt flattered. Girls often liked him but never in a way that made them want to introduce him to their older brothers.

"Just so you know, he's been a bit gloomy lately," she added, her eyes darkening. "It's complicated."

Jim was guessing this had to do with the drug issues Juliet had mentioned to him in the hallway. It was exactly the kind of bombshell his father was probably waiting to get his hands on. Jim wondered how long he could hold off on telling him, while still feeling like a good son. "The drug thing you mentioned?"

"Yes, and just . . . things. I can't really talk about it here." She took Jim's forearm and stepped close to his ear. "With everything going on with James Redmond and the House of Montague, I have to be very careful what I say, in case someone is listening. I never know if the wrong person will use the information against us."

Jim grinned, even as his gut clenched. "Yeah, always best to be careful."

CHAPTER 17

ROMEO

"HOLY SHIT, WOULD you look at the women in here," Benny was yelling unsubtly over the thumping French techno. He banged his head in time with the beat, his eyes almost bursting from their sockets as every new nymphet passed by. "There's no way we go home alone tonight, Romeo."

Romeo looked sideways at Jim, who knew that Romeo didn't want to go home with any of the gyrating sirens who flooded the vast dance floor. Romeo had left a message for Juliet in their secret email, but she'd only written to say that she had to go to a family party that day. She did sign it "love," but he was worried. So he'd invited Jim out with him and Benny tonight, and now realized he hoped for Jim to reassure him that things would be fine with

Juliet. He felt so discombobulated by her long absence—it had been nearly two weeks since they'd touched at the Palais ball—that he was grasping at straws.

The party was Benny's idea. Another warehouse thing in a sketchy part on the edge of the Tenth. Still exclusive, of course. Maybe a harder invite than something more outwardly swank. The guest list boasted a blend of haves like Romeo, Benny, and Jim, and have-lesses, some of whom made up the difference by selling the pills that could make the party fun for people who weren't able to do it on their own. The theme was *Dans les Bois* (French for "Into the Woods") and all around them were girls in various states of au naturel dress. Whether wearing the garb of a woodland sprite, a butterfly, a bird, or a furry mammal, the uniform was similar—bikini tops and hot pants–style bottoms worn with wings or tails and ears of some sort—and lots of body glitter.

The effects on Benny—and most of the guys present, really—was to turn them into wolves on the prowl.

"What? You guys too good for these ladies?" Benny intoned, looking from Romeo to Jim and then back out on the sea of glistening skin. "I suppose you only date big-time models, too." He said it with a sneer toward Jim. So far, Benny had made almost no secret of his distaste for Romeo's new friend. As a loyal lieutenant, Benny was often skeptical of anyone who tried to befriend Romeo, but Jim had the two added annoyances of being someone Romeo actually seemed to like and attracting the attentions of most of the female population at Louis-le-Grand.

"Me? No," Jim said. "Just, you know, sizing up my options." Romeo only knew a little of Jim's romantic past—mostly because the past he had, as Jim told it, wasn't necessarily romantic. In fact, it had been a lot like Romeo's: many seductions but a lack of real feelings.

The guy needed to find his Juliet. Even if Romeo didn't believe many people were able to find their perfect matches the way he had.

A cocktail waitress who definitely wasn't it approached them. The girl was wearing an oversized foxtail and a hat that looked like a fox's head, with long furry extensions falling over her russet bikini. She carried a tray of drinks. Steam seemed to rise from them against the flashing colored lights. "Magic potions, boys?"

"Three," Benny said before asking the others. His gaze sank so far down the girl's top it was a wonder he didn't dive right in.

Romeo pulled out his credit card. Benny had paid the cover and Romeo was used to footing a lot of their entertainment bill. He treated for a great many things.

The waitress tapped the magnetic strip against her iPad, waited a few seconds, then frowned.

"This isn't working," she said, leaning close to Romeo. "Declined."

A declined credit card was so out of the ordinary for Romeo that he didn't for a second think that a real money issue could exist. Thus, he wasn't the least bit embarrassed, the way someone used to watching his spending would be. Jim, too, was unfazed, even knowing as he did that Redmond was looking into the

House of Montague's finances. A life of privilege had the singular disadvantage of putting a person far out of touch with reality.

"I got it," Jim said, handing the waitress his card. The waitress trailed a long-nailed hand down his arm as she lifted the card from his fingertips.

"You certainly do," she said to Jim, who seemed impervious to her woodland-creature charms. Still, he left a sizable tip, Romeo noted. More than Romeo would have, even. He wondered for a second what kind of hostile takeovers Jim's dad specialized in. But what did it matter? Weren't all rich kids the same in a way?

"Thanks for the drink, bro," Benny said, not sounding grateful at all. He took a large swig and excused himself, making his way across the dance floor to talk to a guy in a hooded sweatshirt who was supposed to look like a grizzly bear. No doubt the guy supplied something Benny wanted. Romeo wasn't much for pills and honestly wished his cousin would refrain. But he had other problems: mostly that he felt his only reassurances lately that Juliet still loved him had come through Jim.

"Your cousin's really big on you hooking up with someone," Jim said, offering an appreciative glance at a flock of girls wearing butterfly wings.

"I know," Romeo said. "It's my fault. I used to be quite the collector and Benny got to enjoy the tales."

Jim gestured with his drink toward Benny, dancing wildly in the middle of a circle of girls. "He looks like he'll live," Jim said.

"Yeah . . ." Romeo felt his energy flagging. He'd come tonight to be out and about, and to keep up appearances—for who, exactly, he didn't know. Benny. Bloggers. Women who knew him. He had the wrong kind of reputation to uphold. The only good thing about being here was that at least Jim was aware of his real feelings.

"Wood nymph at twelve o'clock," Jim said, using some Americanism that Romeo wasn't familiar with. Romeo turned to find himself caught in Rosaline's arms, each one wrapped with green silk fashioned to look like climbing vines.

"I heard you were here," Rosaline said, her slithering limbs constricting him on all sides.

The Rosaline conundrum was something he had to address, and soon. The more he was seen with her, the more he feared Juliet would be too angry to bear him.

But she didn't understand that Rosaline was good for their cover. She helped him maintain some sense of his playboy life-style. He didn't want that lifestyle any longer, of course, but what was the harm in being seen with Rosaline to ensure attention stayed off him and Juliet? As long as he didn't mean anything by it, Juliet should have known that she was the one.

"Come dance with me," Rosaline said, skipping off into the throbbing mass of people with a come-hither flick of her wrist.

"I'll be right there," he said.

Jim was looking at him with some kind of macho American squint, as if to say, *What are you doing?*

Romeo didn't acknowledge what he presumed to be a judgment. Instead, he said, "I need a drink."

He ordered another round of drinks and let Jim pay. Among

the very rich, there was often no money-counting (except, of course, when it came time for one party to buy the other party whole).

When the literally foxy waitress had gone, Jim turned to Romeo, who was scouting the dance floor in search of Rosaline.

"I know you have your reasons for the Rosaline thing, but just, you know, be careful with Juliet," Jim shouted over the music.

"I'm nothing but careful with Juliet," Romeo said, irritated. What did Jim know about being in love? The guy had all but admitted he'd never dated anyone seriously. "I would rather be with her. But it'll be a long time before I can change things enough to make our relationship safe."

"Isn't your company being bought?" Jim said. He tossed off the question casually as he held eye contact with an Amazonian girl in an owl costume.

"Since when is that of interest to you?" Romeo shouldn't have been so nasty with Jim. He wasn't mad at him. But he bristled at the sudden interrogation. Wasn't he allowed to blow off steam at a nightclub?

"It was just a question," Jim said. "It's been in the papers. I didn't mean anything by it."

He didn't sound sorry. More annoyed. Romeo realized he was being a prick to Jim. Too much time around Benny and assorted yes-men and now he couldn't handle a few honest questions from someone who wasn't sucking up to him.

"You're right, man," Romeo said, tuning in to the music and his drinks, which were pretty good. He needed this. Between his stressed-out father, Benny constantly hounding him about landing girls, and the fact that he couldn't see his real girlfriend, things hadn't been as effortless for him lately. "I'm just being a dick."

"Nah, it's fine. You're in a hard situation," Jim said. "All I'm saying is that she seemed upset when we talked today. And then when she sees your photo with Rosaline, no matter what I or even you tell her, she'll feel like your relationship isn't real."

"Wait, when did you see her?" Romeo had barely registered anything Jim had said past "we talked today." He could almost imagine the music screeching to a halt. What had Jim been doing with Juliet today—a Saturday? Romeo thought Jim was going to talk to her at school. And that their talk in the halls would be brief and impersonal (or at least only about Romeo).

"It's not a big deal. There was a party for her cousin Thibeau at the house. She invited me, kind of as a cover so her friend Catrine wouldn't—"

He didn't let Jim finish.

"So you were at her house?"

"Yeah," Jim said, while eyeballing another girl across the club. She was dressed in fairy garb and fluttering her long blue eyelashes at him. The Amazonian owl was still watching him, too. Romeo wasn't used to being second fiddle to another guy. "I went to talk to her about you, at school, like we talked about, and she invited me. I mean, it's not weird if I'm friends with both of you, right? We're all friends."

Romeo downed half his drink in one go, feeling the warmth of the whiskey flood his system.

They were all friends but this wouldn't do. He should have been the one at Juliet's house. *He* should be the one seeing her.

"Hey," he asked Jim, feeling seized by an impulse to be with her that went beyond even his normal urge, "do you have Juliet's number?"

"You're dating her, you don't have it?" Jim looked at him like Romeo had just asked him to join a cult.

"No, you know our relationship hasn't been like that," Romeo said, bristling. "I can only reach her through a goddamn secret email account." He knew Jim's question was a reasonable one, but he still didn't like the idea that he was judging them.

But as Jim sent him the number from his own phone, Romeo thought maybe he had been playing things too safe.

He sent her a text message, writing it so she'd know it was from him.

Then he went to join Rosaline on the dance floor.

CHAPTER 18

ROMEO AND JULIET,
TOGETHER AND APART

A TEXT.

Let's meet at our place in the 13th. Noon. A.V.O.

"Who's texting you so early in the morning?" Hélène was an early riser, but until she was out of her robe, she didn't believe the day should start for anyone else. She sipped her café au lait carefully, more to not drive wrinkles into the skin above her lips than to keep from spilling the drink.

In truth, the text had come hours ago, while Juliet slept. And though the number was unfamiliar, she knew at once it was from Romeo. *A.V.O.* gave it away.

Romeo's carelessness was perhaps risky but it was also romantic.

He wanted to see her.

Badly enough that he had texted. No secret email, no notes left on bridges. He'd just been gripped by a need for her and acted. It may have been what she'd wanted all along.

He must have wanted to make sure she saw his message immediately. (She'd never tell him how obsessively she checked their secret email account.)

Juliet turned the phone facedown on the breakfast table and pulled a petal from one of the pink roses from the centerpiece vase. (The Capulets had fresh flowers delivered every other day.)

Turning the velvety petal over in her fingers, thinking, *He loves me*, she told Hélène, "Oh, a friend for a school project. I'll have to go to the *bibliothèque*."

"You can have Guillaume drive you," her father said, not looking up from his tablet, where an array of numbers flooded the small screen. She couldn't tell from his expression if they were good numbers or bad, and right now she didn't care all that much.

Henri could sense something, though, and he raised his eyebrows at her from across the breakfast table. The Capulets didn't eat breakfast together all the time, but the caterers for yesterday's party had sent over a breakfast spread to say thank you, and now the family was nibbling on croissants, a berry tart, and expensive Spanish ham. Juliet could only pick at a croissant. Her body was eager with anticipation.

"I'd better get ready," she said, excusing herself. It was the ideal morning to be in a rush. Hélène would have her aesthetician and masseuse make house calls to rid her of toxins from the party.

And her father would likely be engrossed in work after missing a day of doing it.

Henri followed her to the stairs. "Is it the motorcycle boy?" He wore a grin that indicated he was happy for her. "He's a good-looking guy. I didn't know you went for young street toughs."

She slapped Henri's arm playfully. Her brother was doing much better since his incident, and even though she knew things were always precarious, she was hopeful. "No, it's really a class project." Henri had liked Jim, and vice versa. Juliet wasn't sure if it was Jim's resounding Americanness—so unlike Pierre's more posh ways—that intrigued her brother, or if he just saw that she was comfortable with Jim, but she didn't dare to ask. It was better if her family—even Henri—saw her as their chaste, sweet little girl.

"Okay then," Henri said. "I'm just saying, you getting on the back of a motorcycle would certainly devastate Maman. Don't you remember how upset she was when I took you for your first pair of Doc Martens?"

Juliet laughed, feeling guilty at not letting Henri in on her bigger secret. "I'll keep it in mind," she said, hurrying upstairs to change.

She arrived at the Hotel Lemieux with her backpack slung over her shoulder, and though she'd had a proper shower that morning, Juliet liked the feeling that she might be just another broke and youthful traveler, not a fashion scion who'd been driven halfway here in a dark-windowed Mercedes. (From the library, she'd boarded the Metro.) Her hair was loosely clipped behind her head, and, because of the slight chill in the air, she wore a vintage YSL smoking jacket over a soft white T-shirt and torn jeans.

Mounting the stairs to the second floor, Juliet imagined a scenario wherein Romeo might ask her to run away. In the clothes she was wearing, she felt ready. That she was probably the only potential runaway on earth to own a three-thousand-euro vintage jacket (though she usually could do a lot with very inexpensive finds, she would spend the family money when she thought something was worth it) did not cross her mind.

She knocked once on the door to room 206, where Romeo said he'd be waiting. Like their last time here, Romeo flung the door open almost instantly.

"I had to see you," Romeo said, pulling her into the room and kissing her cheeks, her lips, her neck.

His hands clasped her waist tightly and she pressed her frame against his, burying her nose into the crook of his neck and kissing him there until he let out a low groan.

She ran her hands up his shirt and trailed her fingers down his back. Romeo felt at once that he'd been right to ask for her immediate presence. He couldn't go so long without seeing her.

"I'm so happy to be with you," she said. "I've missed you so much."

Romeo held her at arm's length, even though the energy in the air between them felt like strings that bound them together.

"I more than missed you," he said. "You're all I can think about."

Juliet believed him. She pushed to the back of her mind the questions she had about Rosaline, and about how Romeo spent his time when he wasn't with her. Jim had started to reassure her yesterday and now she was here with Romeo. What proof did she need?

"I've been thinking of you, too," Juliet said, feeling at once at home and confined by the room. In a few hours, they'd have to leave, and she hated how temporary things had to be.

"Yesterday, when Jim said he'd been with you, I wanted to kill him." Romeo was smiling as he said it, but the binding strings felt cut.

Juliet frowned and took a step back from her lover.

"What do you mean, since Jim said he'd been with me?"

"At your house. For your cousin's party." Romeo's mouth pulled down at the corners as he began to wonder whether there was more to the party than Jim had let on. Why would Juliet be upset that he knew?

Walking over to the cracked wood-framed window, he opened it a sliver, letting the air inside. He suddenly felt hot, possibly faint. He looked out at the "courtyard," really just a narrow area where the Dumpsters were housed. Across the way, he could see into the windows of other rooms in the hotel: Three guys passing a joint. A girl painting her toenails. Another couple, embracing.

"So, that is the reason you needed to see me," Juliet said, sitting in the room's somewhat battered chair. The disappointment in her voice was crushing. "Not for me but because you fear Jim."

Romeo continued looking out the window, rather than at her.

Part of him could picture Jim's lips on hers, Jim's arms wrapped around her. . . . Why had such visions come to him so easily? Was there truth to them?

"Should I?" he asked.

Juliet emitted a violent breath and pounded a fist on her knee. "What is wrong with you? You send him to me to tell me that your feelings are real but then you doubt me? He's my friend. He is your friend. You must stop this."

She tightened her lips as she thought of holding on to Jim at the party, pretending to be with him to get rid of Pierre. There'd been a moment when she had enjoyed taking Jim's arm possessively. She'd liked the feel of it beneath her hands. His skin was always warm, even through his clothes. But now she shook the memory away.

"Well, when you're with him and not me, I don't know what to think." Romeo twisted the gold rope curtain tie around his finger, but looked back at her with real concern in his eyes.

Juliet hated him for thinking it but hated herself for enjoying Romeo's jealousy. She'd had so much envy to contend with, not just from the photos of him with Rosaline at the Palais event but also from her knowledge that Romeo had been with plenty of women before her. He was her first and only—even her first kiss—while he'd admitted to filling a box with souvenirs of his conquests. He may have burned it, but that didn't mean those dalliances had never happened.

She always wondered, could she really compete?

But now, wasn't he telling her that she'd won?

"If the only way for you to need me is to make you doubt me, then this is not the love we believed, is it?" Juliet said, softly. She wanted to provoke him.

Romeo turned from the window swiftly, trying to hide the hurt in his eyes. "I always need you. And I trust in you. I hate that he can be with you in the daylight, at your home, with your family, while I can only be with you here." It was true, but saying it aloud rattled him for how much he meant it. If he lost Juliet, it might break him.

Her body flooded with warmth. She'd wanted, so badly, to know that she mattered to him, had the power to hurt him, even though she never wanted to cause him pain. "That's what I've been saying, my love," she said. "We deserve to be part of the world, not hiding from it."

Romeo ran a hand through his longish hair. "You know why we can't," he said. "You know with this Redmond thing, everything is harder than ever. My father doesn't trust anyone right now. If he knew I was with you, he wouldn't trust me, either. I'd be cut out."

Since giving the speech at the shareholders' meeting and Henri's incident, Juliet had felt more keenly what concerned Romeo. She still was not in total agreement, but she better understood his reasons for being the way he was. Who they were *did* matter.

"We don't need to talk about that now," she said.

Juliet crossed to the window, slipping out of her jacket as she did so. She threw it carelessly over the lumpy upholstered chair, then pulled her T-shirt over her head. She slipped out of her jeans just as fluidly and stood before Romeo, naked save for her delicate white underthings.

"I have nothing to hide from you," she told him, taking his hands in hers. "Let me prove it."

CHAPTER 19

ROMEO

"IS THAT A taxidermied rat dressed as Louis the Fourteenth?" Jim asked, pointing at a rat that was indeed wearing a brocade robe and carrying a golden walking stick. It stood upright, posed with one hand on its hip like it had important king business to do.

"Yes, of course," Juliet said. "What, they don't dress up dead rats in your country?" Romeo belted out a laugh. Last week's meeting at Hotel Lemieux had repaired things between him and Juliet, and today she'd suggested she get out of her house using the fake-school-project ruse again. She'd said they should bring along Jim. Romeo knew she'd said it to keep him from wondering about their relationship, but Juliet hadn't put it that way, and he loved her all the more for it. She made even the hard things easy.

"I thought the French were supposed to have taste," Jim said, still regarding the animal quizzically. "That looks like something I could get in Alabama from someone who married their cousin. A keen eye, but still."

"Whatever, rich boy," Romeo said. "As if you'd shop at a store in Alabama. We all know you bought your jacket already beat-up from the Dolce and Gabbana flagship."

"Touché," Jim said, clutching his arm as if wounded by a sword. "It's Gucci and I had them messenger it over, but you're close."

As Romeo waved off a woman trying to sell him a paisley scarf, he wondered, how could he have been jealous?

If there were something to be jealous of with Juliet and Jim, they'd never have both been here. Juliet loved him, not Jim, and the three of them were friends, just like she'd said.

Juliet loved vintage shopping and had wanted to come here, to Les Puces, called the Queen of Flea, in the Twentieth. It was the world's biggest flea market, and the perfect place to not be noticed, given the three thousand stalls and crowds of people too busy scouring the wares for a bizarre treasure to be paying much attention to them.

"I need to get away from these dead animals," Juliet said, dashing ahead of them to a stall filled with old sunglasses, scarves, and hats. "Come on."

She immediately found a men's black fedora and a pair of oversized mirrored glasses. Bundling her hair atop her head, she placed the hat over it and tried on the sunglasses, which were far too big for her face, but that drew Romeo's eyes straight to her bee-stung lips.

"You know," she said, curving those lips in a mischievous smile, "we should have disguises."

She started to root through a box of secondhand scarves, all of which had that dusty thrift-store smell. How was it that people could smell so different but their used clothing smelled the same?

"I thought the whole point of coming here was that we wouldn't need them," Romeo said, politely shaking his head as he was approached by a small woman in a loose flower-print dress selling cell phone cases and knock-off Hello Kitty keychains. Even in Paris, there was a market for cheaply made Chinese crap, and for whatever reason, Romeo must have looked like the kind of rich sucker who would hand out euros just to get merchants off his back.

"It's more fun if we have disguises, though," Juliet said, a strand of her hair falling from the hat and curling around her cheek. Her grin persisted in its infectiousness. And while Romeo loathed the part of their relationship that made the disguises seem like the right idea, he secretly saw a practicality to it. Juliet might have thought they were safe here, but really, you couldn't trust any situation. He wouldn't tell her that today. He knew how she hated being reminded of his practical concerns, and he'd stopped himself from pointing out the glances they'd received. The eyes of onlookers made him nervous and he had to tell himself they might just be admiring Juliet's beauty, not recognizing who she was.

So, yes, disguises might put him at ease. Because right now, he was enjoying himself, and enjoying being out in public with her—his girlfriend—and with Jim, his friend. He really did like having someone he could trust with his Juliet secret. Someone who, unlike Benny, wouldn't push for sordid details. And who he knew respected the relationship.

His phone buzzed in his pocket. He took it out and saw Rosaline's number, along with a string of X's and O's and a photo of her in a bikini so stylized that it had to be from the fashion shoot she'd mentioned at the party last week.

He'd screwed up there. He'd been so worked up—and had drunk so much—that he'd danced with Rosaline most of the night. He'd kissed her, just for show. But now she had been trying to arrange a date, and he couldn't completely blow her off since she was one of Montague's lead models for the next two seasons. She had amazing business acumen—she'd turned a Kate Moss–style drug problem into more modeling contracts and a successful life-coaching enterprise—and Romeo's father thought the world of her. He would have loved to see Romeo paired off with her in a corporate coup to rub in the faces of the competition, take over social media, and help sales return to what Jean Montague called the "glory days," when he was first dating Romeo's mother.

"What's that?" Jim said quietly, startling Romeo. But Juliet didn't hear him, as she was still going through the used clothing.

"Rosaline," Romeo said, deleting the message and shaking his head. "I need to extricate myself from that situation."

"You do," Jim said. "But not right now."

See, he was a friend. A guy after your girlfriend would have made sure she knew about your too-close-for-comfort moments with another woman. Romeo told himself he'd been his own worst enemy, thinking he had something to fear with Juliet and Jim being friends.

Jim started rooting through a bucket of hats and pulled one out to try on. It was an old-school biker hat that made him look like a young Marlon Brando, especially when worn with his leather jacket.

"I like this," Jim said, not hiding that he was admiring himself in the mirror.

Romeo squelched the voice in the back of his head that wondered if Juliet thought Jim looked as good as Jim seemed to think he did.

"I'll do this one," Romeo said, choosing a knit skullcap that gave him a thuggish vibe, as Benny would say, along with a pair of dark glasses that made his light hair look even lighter. He wasn't sure if he looked dangerous or like some skinny poet with consumption and not enough time outdoors.

Juliet stood on her tiptoes to kiss him. "You are so handsome, *mon amour.*"

"Yes, *mon amour,*" Jim echoed in a teasing voice. "You look like someone who might steal my wallet."

"And you look like someone showing up for their first day of motorcycle school."

Jim laughed and raised a middle finger in a jovial manner.

"Aww," Juliet said, putting an arm around Jim in a purely friendly way. "But he looks handsome, too. Like Steve McQueen."

Steve McQueen . . . was he better-looking than Brando? Was he the one who died young? And Brando was the one who got fat.

Romeo checked his reflection. He wasn't a rugged motorcycle guy. He was almost pretty, like a young Leo DiCaprio.

When Juliet let go of Jim, Romeo wrapped his arms around her waist from behind and pulled her into him. He kissed the back of her neck, the skin that had been exposed when she'd put her hair up.

She sighed with pleasure.

If he knew she was his, why did he so frequently feel the need to prove it?

CHAPTER 20

JIM

"I'M STARVING," **JIM** heard himself say. He wasn't really, but trailing after Romeo and Juliet as they held hands was starting to wear on him. They weren't treating him like a third wheel, not exactly, but when you were the third wheel you felt like one. And even though Les Puces was huge—they'd probably seen only a quarter of the vendors, if that—it was starting to feel repetitive. He wasn't much of a shopper to begin with, and he had no use for the handmade soaps or bohemian-looking jewelry. He wasn't even in the mood to chat anyone up, though he'd seen a few cute girls here and there.

"Yeah, food would be good," Romeo said, looping his arm over Juliet's shoulder and pulling her close. Again. "What about you, Madeline?" He used the fake name Juliet said went with her disguise. Jim thought she looked more like a Billie, one of those rare girls who can adopt a guy's name and make it that perfect mix of feminine and spunky.

Juliet-Madeline-Billie nodded, and leaned her head against Romeo's shoulder. Just like that Bob Dylan album with the famous cover. Jim had never listened to the album, but had always liked the cover.

Romeo guided Juliet toward a small café on the Avenue de Saint-Ouen. Despite France's reputation as a food mecca, Jim had discovered plenty of places like this, cafés that were something between a diner and a bistro, where the food was the definition of "fine"—satisfying but not necessarily memorable. He'd guess Romeo had been to a few, on nights out with his guy friends, but Juliet's more limited experience brought her to nicer places with her family.

Jim was always guessing things about them. What did he really know? Maybe his friendship was just a novelty for them. Some token American they could hang out with for a few months and then abandon.

Maybe he just had a crush on them.

He was used to being the new guy with a crowd of admirers everywhere he went. In Paris, he was starting to feel like his fish-out-of-water status was what made him so intent on securing Romeo and Juliet's friendship, instead of the other way around.

Was it the way they'd met that first day that gave Jim the sense he had a bond with them, or was it just a little different here in

Paris? Normally, other rich kids at his boarding schools seemed so intent on impressing each other. Everything was a social climb, even though they were all at the top. Romeo and Juliet weren't like that. It was why he felt like their friendship was more real.

He reminded himself that he wasn't even supposed to be taking the friendship thing seriously. This was just a job, a mission for his dad. He had yet to give his dad any details, partly because his father hadn't been home much. Still, he couldn't imagine what he wanted to tell his father about his friends. He was starting to wish he'd just met them and befriended them naturally, somehow. He didn't want to sell them out, but he feared—almost knew—that he eventually would. No one held out on James Redmond forever.

Yet, every moment he spent with them, the more he felt like he was betraying everyone, himself maybe most of all. He felt especially confused about Juliet, if he was being honest. He wanted to not care so much when she laughed at one of his jokes or teased him about his American ways, but the truth was, she delighted him. But she was Romeo's girl. Even if Jim had been a little disgusted by the scene Romeo had made with Rosaline the other night, there was a code with guys. Plus, he knew that Romeo was only with the model to keep up appearances. Or, at least to hear Romeo tell it, that was the reason.

Romeo was already requesting a table when Jim asked, "Do they have anything for Juliet?"

He thought Juliet would look grateful that he'd remembered.

Instead, she looked at him like a teenager who just got told she had to eat at the kids' table.

Like a girl who wanted to speak for herself.

Jim felt instantly like an ass. What was his goal anyway?

Still, he looked at Romeo, wanting to see how he'd respond.

"What do you mean?" Romeo asked. "They have everything." He gestured to a passing tray laden with sandwiches and a steak.

"She doesn't eat meat, just fish," Jim said. He realized he was trying to mark territory, and he didn't know why it was important to him. "I saw some sushi places back there."

He gestured to the route they'd taken. Japanese food was evidently big in the Montmartre neighborhood.

Romeo looked from Jim to Juliet and back to Jim.

"Oh, yeah, I know she doesn't," Romeo said. "This place has a *baguette fromage.*"

Jim cringed, wondering why he'd pushed the issue. It was like he had a subconscious need to show himself the better of the two boys for Juliet. That kind of stuff had been fine back at boarding school, to get some other guy's girlfriend. But he told himself he wasn't going to steal Juliet. He just had some kind of biological programming to be an overstepping dick. *Thanks a lot, Dad*, he thought.

"And I can order for myself," Juliet said, not looking upset anymore. With a skip in her step, she traipsed past the two boys as they avoided eye contact and read the menu posted on the sidewalk. "I just want a giant plate of fries anyway. Let's go."

Romeo gave Jim a strange look as he walked inside. "You okay, man? You're acting kind of weird."

Jim forced a grin. "Yeah, just hungry. I'll be fine."

He wondered if anyone had ever made that same promise and believed it.

CHAPTER 21

JULIET

"I WANT TO do something silly, that all the tourists do." She'd devoured half the plate of fries already, and dipped several more into the creamy Mornay sauce that accompanied them. Sometimes, the perfect junk food was better than the best gourmet meal.

It was the same way the silly randomness of the day was almost superior to the romance of meeting Romeo for a secret tryst. Almost. But she loved this—the flea market, the disguises, the laughing at everything, the irresponsible eating. It was nice to feel like a normal teenager. No Gabrielle talking about some fabulous party, no awkward conversation with Pierre as her mother lingered, no trying to be genuine with Margaux and Catrine.

The only other time she felt so at ease was with Henri, on his good days. Well, and with Romeo, but that required so many steps to stay protected. But now, she was a normal girl, Madeline, with her boyfriend. And their friend. Jim.

Maybe it had been another intervention of fate that had brought Jim into their lives. Would they ever be out like this if it weren't for him?

Even Hélène had been happy, when Juliet said she'd be spending the day with Jim. "The American from the party?" She'd looked at Juliet with something like respect. "Fair enough. If Pierre calls, I will tell him you're out." For Hélène, that was a huge compliment to Jim. Juliet suspected that Jim appealed to Hélène for the same reasons Hélène had picked Juliet's father, Maurice: He seemed like someone who could protect a woman. Not that Juliet believed she needed protecting, but she knew how her mother's primal needs emerged.

"Moulin Rouge?" Romeo suggested, spinning a straw on the table. "That's touristy."

"*Non,*" Juliet said. "You'll get too uncomfortable if you think people are watching us instead of them." She knew it was true and she found she wasn't mad, this time. Maybe because she felt more like Romeo's true love today than ever before. The secret meetings at the hotel had their good points, of course, but this open-air courtship was what she'd wanted, at least part of the time.

"Catacombs?" Jim offered, scrolling through a list of places on his phone. "Touristy and creepy."

She shook her head. "Somewhere aboveground."

"Notre-Dame? Our church?" Romeo raised an eyebrow as Jim looked from him to her with a question in his eyes.

"Your church?" Jim asked, holding his burger in midair.

"We pass notes near there, meeting places on the Love-Lock Bridge," Romeo whispered. His skullcap was still pulled low over his forehead, and he'd tucked his longish blond hair under it. Juliet loved his hair and his fine features but liked that he looked a little tough in that hat. Maybe she shared some primal needs with her mother.

"*Non*, the Eiffel Tower," Juliet said, seeing Jim's slight frown, and deciding not to think about it. She pointed toward the ever-present landmark in the distance.

"Well, I've never been," Jim said. "I'm in."

Romeo grinned. "Sounds perfect."

An hour, two Metro transfers, and a line full of tourists later, they were in the elevator, on the way to the top of the Eiffel Tower. Juliet realized she hadn't been since a trip with her tutor when she was twelve. Romeo, too, was looking around in wonder. And Jim stared out over the city like he was Rip Van Winkle, asleep for half his life and just waking up to a world that had grown more complex in his absence.

It was dusk, and Paris resembled an artistic dessert at the end of a perfect meal. A feathery pink light dappled the streets below, each building an ivory confection with glowing windows.

What might have been as amazing as all of Paris shimmering below was that no one looked twice at them. The flow of tourists—some in gawky white sneakers, others in flowing lin-ens, plenty carrying shopping bags (many from the Montague and Capulet flagship stores on the Champs-Élysées), and nearly all of them snapping selfies on the way up—meant that every-one was so wrapped up in their own stories that they had no time for (or no knowledge of) the one between Romeo and Juliet. And Jim. He was part of this now, too.

When the doors opened at the top, a gust of cool air greeted them and Juliet tilted her head back, loving the way it felt on her skin.

"Why don't I come up here more often?" she said. This was what people meant when they said "living in the moment." Prone as she sometimes was to worrying about what had been and what would be, she didn't feel any of that now. From up here, every-thing looked small enough to manage. From up here, she could see her home on Avenue Montaigne and Romeo's just blocks down the street. Long ago, as the homes were being built, some ancient, angry Capulet had watched the Montague house go up, waiting long enough to make sure the Capulet manse was just a meter wider, a fact that Romeo had once told her still bothered his father. From up here, though, the homes looked exactly the same.

Romeo and Jim had gone to the railing along the observation deck. A chain-link fence guarded against people jumping off, but it was easily ignored. Both boys looked like the epitome of con-templative. She wondered what they thought about, and tried to imagine them as men. She realized she loved them both, just in different ways.

"Let's yell something off the top," Juliet said, stepping in between the boys and putting her left hand on Romeo's right wrist and her right hand on Jim's left.

Jim and Romeo turned to look at her and then at each other. "What are you talking about?"

"I don't know," Juliet said, more seized by the idea by the second. "I just want to do it—like what if we say, 'We are young! We are alive!' "

It was the urge to be loud that appealed to her most. Her whole life, she'd been behaving, and even now her biggest misbehaviors had to be kept secret. She was always polite, smart but never calling too much attention to it, never one to rock the boat.

But the boys weren't excited by the idea. They were still looking at her like they were glad the fence was there to keep her from jumping.

"Please," Juliet said. "Doesn't it seem like something they'd do in a movie?"

Jim rolled his eyes at Romeo.

"Yeah, some awful American movie where the poor inner-city school kids win a spelling bee and get a trip to Paris instead of, you know, new textbooks or something they actually need," Jim said in a deadpan voice.

"I'm with Jim," Romeo said. "It won't be good. It will be lame."

"I'd rather be lame and happy than look cool and be miserable," she said. "You're both just scared."

That comment got them.

"Fine, whatever, we can do it," Jim said. "Right?"

Romeo nodded. "Yeah, I'm not scared," he said. "I don't get it, but I'm not afraid." He wove his fingers with hers and squeezed her hand.

"Well?" She offered a hand to Jim, who took her palm into his.

"I'll start," she said. People milled around them, snapping photos and gazing at the city, but she didn't feel strange.

"WE ARE YOUNG!" Her voice wasn't as strong as she'd hoped it would be—maybe she was a little nervous. A petite Asian woman in skyscraper-tall heels glanced at her but smiled benignly.

She pulled off the fedora and let her waves tumble down. The wind whipped her hair around her face.

"Say it with me this time," she said to the boys.

This time, neither Romeo nor Jim protested.

"WE ARE YOUNG!"

Her voice was the loudest but she could see the boys grin as they heard their own voices echo out over the city.

"WE ARE ALIVE!"

They yelled it three times, and with each repetition, Romeo and Jim looked as inspired as she felt. They *were* young. They *were* alive. They were happy.

With a grin toward Romeo, she added one more significant phrase.

"AMOR VINCIT OMNIA!"

Love conquers all.

She knew she was right.

CHAPTER 22

JIM

JIM WALKED INTO what he figured to be an empty apartment
and he was . . .

. . . happy.

Yes, Juliet was, maybe, the first girl he'd ever met who he felt
utterly beguiled by. But also maybe the first one he ever thought
he could be friends with. He was at home with her.

As he was with Romeo. He'd been friends with other simi-
larly rich boys before, but with them, everything was a pissing
contest.

Sometime while they were at the top of the Eiffel Tower, he'd
decided that he needed to put aside any longing he had for Juliet
and instead enjoy the friendship. If he had a therapist, they'd no

doubt say that his conflicting emotions toward her stemmed from his joint feelings of love and anger toward his mother, because he was still carrying the weight of her suicide.

Figuring himself to know better than any therapist was exactly why he'd always turned down offers and prescriptions to have one. He'd had to go to one after getting kicked out of Choate, for what had been called "self-destructive behavior" (he called it a finals-missing bender), but that hadn't gone so well. The therapist had proven excessively hot and just on the right side of crazy to hook up with Jim. Now he knew what the couches were for.

Right now, he'd say he didn't need a shrink because he felt at home. Or, at home when he wasn't here, at his actual supposed home. This apartment felt assuredly like his father's home, not Jim's. The fact that the furnishings changed overnight with no input from his father honestly made the place more representative of James Redmond than less. Personal expression, to Jim's father, was a waste of time. Keeping someone on the payroll as a corporate tax write-off, however, was very in line with his personality.

"Have a nice day?"

When his father's voice came from the kitchen, Jim flinched.

No, almost jumped.

"Yeah, I did," he said honestly, even as his gut churned with worry his dad would ask how the "mission" was going.

"Want a beer?"

"Sure, yeah, that would be great," Jim said, answering in the affirmative multiple times because he was so thrown off by his dad's sudden offer. He stepped through the living room to the kitchen, where his dad actually pushed a bottle of beer across the counter to him. Kronenbourg 1664.

Jim picked up the frosty bottle and took a long pull, surprised to see his dad home and maybe more surprised to have his dad talking to him.

"Wonder if that's what Ben Franklin drank when he was here, catching syphilis from French whores," his father said. He poured his own beer into a glass and offered one to Jim, who was already half done with the bottle.

Jim waved off the glass and laughed. His father had almost never referred to sex in conversation with him in his life. And he'd gone straight for the joke about prostitutes and STDs and a guy in a wig. Maybe his dad was not always so serious. "Franklin had syphilis?"

His father grinned and shook his head. "I thought that was the going knowledge. What are they teaching you in that school? I thought it was one of the best in Europe, and they can't even tell you the activities of our dead statesmen?"

It was rare for his father to joke. No, it was unheard of. He must have been in a very good mood. Or maybe this was the start of some kind of mental breakdown.

"Did you have a good day?" Jim asked. If his father asked about how Jim's snooping was going, he decided he could tell him something. Something small, though, that didn't reveal anything too damaging. Maybe just that Romeo's relationship with Rosaline seemed phony. That wouldn't hurt anyone, right?

Or maybe his dad had forgotten the assignment altogether. Maybe he had enough ducks in a row. Better yet, maybe he'd found something else to buy and merge that didn't involve the families of Jim's first real friends . . . ever.

His dad patted a ream of papers on the counter. "Yes," he said. "My clever acquaintance has proved useful at digging into the financial data on our friends the Montagues and Capulets."

"Oh, really?" He found himself thinking of his friends and the easy way they went through life, like him. He wasn't stupid; he knew money made things that way. If you could pay for all the things you wanted, you could make your worst problems the ones inside your own heart. It was part luxury, part price you paid. Sometimes, it seemed like being poor would be easier. At least when you're going hungry, you know exactly what your problem is.

"Yes, all's not well there," his dad said. "I'll have to keep you posted."

"Me?"

"Of course. It's your company, too. We're in this together." His dad said it like it was a truth as unworthy of mentioning as other taken-for-granted facts like a live-in housekeeper fixing the beds each morning. But "we're in this together"? James Redmond only said the word *together* when he wanted to take over more than one company at a time, the way he was with the houses of Montague and Capulet.

His dad took a sip of his beer and peered at his phone. "So, how has your fact-finding mission been going?"

To shrug and say nothing would probably mean his father's sudden interest in him would retreat just as quickly as it had surged. But what would saying more mean?

"Um, you know, it's um . . ." Jim took another swig from his beer.

His dad's face clouded over. "Hmmph," he snorted.

"What is it?" Jim asked, knowing that the answer was a litany of fatherly disappointment that fit neatly into "hmmph."

His dad shrugged. "Oh, I don't know," he said. "I suppose I was too impressed by your trailing them. I should have guessed you'd get distracted by whatever it is you do."

Now his father looked away, sipping his beer like he wished he were somewhere else, with a better son.

"You know, I think they might be dating," Jim blurted out, wanting to prove his dad wrong. He *had* gotten information.

He regretted it the instant he said it. And as soon as the guilt coursed through him, he started to rationalize revealing such a huge detail. He tried to tell himself it was a strategic move. It was noncommittal—he'd just said they *might* be dating—and he hadn't given up anything about where they'd been or things they'd said about their parents. Really, what harm could actually come of their dating? How could two high school students being a couple amount to anything real in this world of his father's? At least he hadn't spilled what he knew about Henri's drug problem.

He knew, though, that his motivation for revealing the Romeo and Juliet fact was Psychology 101: He wanted his father's approval. *And* he wanted Juliet and hoped that blowing their cover would break them apart. But he now regretted the sub-conscious selfishness.

Because his dad looked like a hungry tiger at the zoo who'd just been thrown a hunk of bloody meat.

"Hmm, that's extremely interesting."

"Why?" Jim asked, now feeling panicked. He could hear the edge in his voice, so he adjusted his question. "I mean, how would teenagers dating really matter to the businesses?" He desperately wanted it to not really matter. Romeo was his first real friend, and Juliet . . . well, he never wanted to hurt her. Or did he? Sometimes, he thought it would be nice if he could trade places with one of them, either of them, instead of being the conflicted son with the dead mom and the uncaring dad, who was trying so hard to make everything work out.

His dad grinned. He wasn't a smiler, so he wore it about as comfortably as he would a Santa Claus suit in June. "Those families have been enemies for more than a century," he said. "Their mutual hatred is governed by laws I don't even fully understand yet. And besides, anytime two enemies are in bed together, they shrink in scope. It's easier to move them around when they're bound together. Really good work, son."

The effect of being called "son" was as pride-inducing as the sense of having put his friends in danger was guilt-inducing. Turmoil mingled with the beer and his empty stomach. He hadn't eaten since the café near Les Puces.

"Have you had dinner?" his dad asked, bringing Jim back to the present.

"Not yet."

"Come on. I'm joining Jennifer tonight," his dad said. "She wants to eat at the restaurant in that tin thing."

He waved toward the Eiffel Tower out the window. Its lights were ablaze, casting little rays of gold into the darkening sky.

The irony was not lost on Jim that he and his father were joining Jennifer at the place where he'd only hours before been with the friends he may have just betrayed.

"Jennifer really wanted to eat here?" Jim asked. It wasn't that the Eiffel Tower restaurant wasn't nice. It was, very. Jim just thought Jennifer would want to dine somewhere exclusive and hidden that no one knew about but that she would tell them about. Somewhere where everyone was a little mean, like she was.

James Redmond smirked. "I think even the most cutthroat of women can't resist the Eiffel Tower. I don't get it, but I suppose it is iconic."

They had a table near the window, probably the best one in the place. They sat down and ordered a bottle of wine—his dad chose it. He even asked about the humidity in the Loire Valley three years ago, as if he knew anything about what humidity meant for grapes. Jim didn't think his dad had been outside in years, much less somewhere where things grew. But the sommelier answered deferentially and did that thing they did in movies, where he poured it and let his dad sniff it, then taste it, then nod approvingly. Jim wondered if his father really knew anything about wine.

But then James Redmond held his glass aloft and said, "To

family. I realize I haven't always been the father you've needed, but just know I didn't have the best example."

"Fair enough," Jim said, not really knowing what else to say. His dad had never said *I love you*. They'd never played catch. Between his mother's suicide and his father's utter lack of affection, Jim was sometimes amazed that he wasn't a serial killer. Though maybe you grew into that, he joked darkly to himself. To be fair, maybe his dad was due some compassion after being left as an orphan at a convent in New Orleans. "That means a lot," he corrected himself.

It did mean a lot.

Jim took a sip of the wine, thinking it was good and this was good. He just wanted a way to keep his dad like this—acting almost like his dad—while still being friends with Romeo and Juliet.

He could do that, couldn't he?

"Jennifer is coming, right?" he asked, not looking up from the menu. Could some of this newfound-father stuff be a softer side spurred on by his dad marrying Jennifer? Jim thought of the weird seduction test Jennifer had put him through. It wasn't the best way to bond with your new stepmother, but then, it wasn't like Jim had a lot of options in the family realm.

"She'll be along."

Jim skipped past the escargot and duck leg confit listed on the menu, just wanting a big steak. He wanted to fill the hollow pit in his stomach that ached with anxiety.

"God, I could really use a good steak," his dad said, prompting Jim to think that maybe he really was his father's son after all.

Jim had set his menu down and was about to say he wanted the same thing when a camera flash lit his peripheral vision. He turned to see a photographer snapping a shot of him and his dad. "Hey," he said, on the defensive until he saw Jennifer strutting up behind the photographer.

"Let's get another one of the toast," she said. She smiled at Jim. "Hi, Jim. Can you pick up your wineglass again? Neither of you have to say anything this time. Davide was late." This she said with a scowl at the offending photographer, who was French enough to not care what Jennifer thought of him.

"What are these for?" Jim asked. He didn't mind. It was just weird. The last time he and his father had been photographed together was probably when he was a little kid and they'd been getting out of the car for his mother's funeral.

"Just to have for the business. Posterity," Jennifer said. "It's your company, too."

His dad nodded, holding his own wineglass aloft for what was sure to be a cheesy photo. "Like I said."

Jim smiled and did as he was told, holding up his glass and pretending to be absorbed by his father's toast, even though his dad was just asking Jennifer if certain figures had come in on some Japanese deal.

After Davide had snapped many shots, Jennifer sat down and poured herself a glass of the wine. She made her own toast. "To the Redmond men."

Jim couldn't tell from the way she said it if the toast was one for business or for pleasure. Of course, if she was going to be his new stepmom, the transaction was probably a little of both. More business, knowing his dad.

Davide kept snapping shots as Jennifer pulled a tablet from her bag and started swiping into a program.

The other diners were watching them now. A dinner in the Eiffel Tower clearly meant more to most of them than it did to Jennifer, who'd barely glanced out the window.

"I thought you wanted to take in the view," Jim's dad said to Jennifer. But it was obvious that they were the same kind of person, because as Jennifer pulled up the Japanese deal numbers, his dad leaned toward her, looking at a spreadsheet like it was far prettier than anything in the city below.

He wondered why he wanted his dad's attention so much, when it was clear that James Redmond paid attention to the wrong things.

But he sat still, ordered his food, and smiled when his father or Jennifer tried a joke about some business deal or other that made no sense to him.

Just hours ago, yelling off the top of this very tower, he'd never felt more like he knew his place in the world.

He'd felt young and alive and certain.

But now . . . He was young. He was alive.

And he was lost.

CHAPTER 23

JULIET

SHE'D WANTED TO be Madeline again today but it was not in the cards. There was actual homework to catch up on, and she was staying around the house with a hidden goal of checking on Henri, just to make sure things were really okay. Since Thibeau's party last week, she'd barely seen her brother. She'd been at school, he'd had "appointments," and their paths hadn't crossed. In truth, she knew she'd been in her Romeo-daydream bubble. Believing Henri was fine because he'd been fine at the party was a trap that was too easy to fall into. She needed verification.

But even as the housekeepers, cooks, personal shoppers, and sundry other assistants funneled in and out downstairs, Juliet's home felt big and empty and void of possibilities. She rolled over in bed, wishing for some new option to present itself.

She could have invited friends over. Even Jim, who now knew her family. But Jim, well, she didn't know what he did on the weekends exactly, but she sensed she shouldn't ask him to hang out with her on his own. Most of the time when the three of them had been together, things had been fine, but here and there, she caught herself wondering if Jim looked at her too long, or made a show of looking away when Romeo kissed her. And the thing at the café, like he was testing Romeo's knowledge of all things Juliet, that had been odd.

She liked when it was the three of them. There was safety in numbers, probably.

So, schoolwork. She'd been on a high since the previous weekend, and her focus had been a touch shot. She was way behind on her Balzac paper, and her chemistry labwork was just a series of scribbles.

Ugh. Couldn't homework wait? Right now, maybe what she wanted was Truffaut in the screening room. She'd ease into the harder stuff.

She was halfway into a favorite when her phone screen lit up. Gabrielle. It read, *Did I show you this outfit? (PMS-y, I need attention.)*

It was an image of Gabrielle at a party of some sort, dressed in what could only be described as a sexy owl costume. But it wasn't Gabrielle's outfit that caught her eye. Behind Gabrielle, Juliet saw the unmistakable form of Rosaline, dancing with

Romeo. And not the formal dance from the Palais fashion gala. This was writhing. Romeo's head was tilted back in what looked like ecstasy.

Juliet texted, her fingers trembling: *When was this?*

Gabrielle texted the date of Thibeau's party. The night before she'd been with Romeo at Hotel Lemieux. Just last week, when everything had seemed perfect again.

Juliet punched her fist into the couch cushion as *Jules et Jim* continued to unspool on the screen behind her. Her attention had been shattered by this. She slapped the cushions again and again, her hair whipping around her face, but it wasn't enough: She felt capable of burning down the world around her.

Should she call him, write him, go over to his house and slap him?

No. He'd just say the same thing he always did and would— that he had to. Yes, he just *had* to dance with a model like a dance in the bedroom was next.

No, he couldn't chalk this one up to something his parents had required.

She didn't even hear Henri come up behind her.

"What's that?" He picked up her phone from where she'd tossed it onto the cushion. She lunged for it, not knowing why. What difference did it make now if Henri knew? What difference would it ever have made?

"Gabrielle?" He looked up at her with concerned eyes.

"Yes, just some silly photo Gabrielle sent from a party." She tried to toss off the words casually but her voice caught on "party."

"Who's this in the back?" Henri's eyes flashed in the dark. She couldn't get a good look at them to see if he looked high. She was too wrapped up in her own problems to care right now.

But *A.V.O.* Didn't it go back to that? Wasn't that how she knew Rosaline was just a blip on the eternal timeline she and Romeo would have?

Or was that just a handy phrase Romeo could use anytime she was mad?

"You and Romeo," Henri said. "I always suspected."

She'd forgotten her brother was here. How did he know? Juliet felt horror curl up her arms and legs and in her stomach, but instead of denying anything to Henri, she grabbed his arm and said, "You can't tell Maman. Or Papa."

Henri put his hands on his hips and looked at her for a long time. Anger mounted in her heart. Was he really going to out her? After what she'd done for him?

"Juliet, what on earth would make you think I'd do that?" Now he sat down on the couch and patted the seat next to him. As Juliet sat, he looped an arm over her shoulder, squeezing her tight. When they were little, it was Henri's go-to pose for family photos. After all these moments worrying about him, she realized she hadn't felt like the little sister in some time. But now, at least, her big brother was back.

Juliet shrugged beneath his arm. *"Je ne sais pas."*

Henri fumbled in his shirt pocket for his cigarette case. He lit two and gave her one. She inhaled deeply. Juliet didn't smoke often, but she was French and a Frenchwoman amid personal disaster didn't fall apart outwardly; instead she inhaled her darkness via the Gauloise and let it fill the void left by a heartbreak. (And, yes, Frenchwomen were also dramatic.)

Watching the smoke curl up toward the ceiling, she asked, "How did you know?"

Henri smiled wanly. "I saw the way you looked at him at the Palais party. When you were stuck with Pierre."

Juliet let out an ironic laugh. She'd thought she'd been so clever.

"I don't judge you," he said. "But know this. He is a drug. Your drug."

The orange embers of her cigarette crackled in the darkened room. "Isn't all love a drug?"

Henri nodded as he picked up the remote and paused the Truffaut film on a scene of Jules and Jim leaning into each other. "Yes and no. When you can't have someone all the time, the moments with them are the high, and the moments without them are the despair when you can think of nothing but them."

He wasn't wrong. She almost wished Henri had wanted to out her love affair to their parents. Him telling her the truth was far and away worse.

Juliet did despair when she wasn't with Romeo, couldn't talk to him, couldn't hear from him, couldn't have him. But she'd never before thought that was something to blame Romeo for. It was their situation and the circumstances that caused it. Not Romeo himself.

But maybe she'd been lying to herself this whole time.

Didn't she deserve to be wanted and craved and sought? Why should she obsess over someone who wasn't obsessing over her?

She squeezed her brother's hand. She was restless and the room suddenly felt like it fit her uncomfortably, like a shoddy pair of jeans that had been cut incorrectly. "Thank you, *mon frère*." She rose to leave.

"Where are you going? We can finish the movie," Henri said. He looked hopeful, like he wanted her to stay. But she couldn't.

Or she wouldn't.

"I just need some air."

She texted Jim: *Can we go out on your motorcycle?*

She didn't know why she didn't text Romeo instead. Maybe she just wanted to prove he wasn't her drug, that he was a habit she could quit. She tried to rationalize texting Jim instead of confronting Romeo. But the truth was, she just wanted to see him. Jim. As much as, maybe more than, she wanted to see Romeo right now.

Jim didn't ask questions, just said yes.

He arrived within a half hour. Juliet hadn't changed her clothes since the morning. She'd cried away her makeup and her eyes were puffy. She didn't really care.

"Maman," she called, and then waited. . . .

Hélène emerged from her parlor, with Serge and Patric, her beauty techs, in tow. "Juliet, I was just thinking that maybe you'd like to do something with your hair . . ." She trailed off, seeing Jim in his leather jacket, standing in the entryway.

"I'm going out," Juliet said, wanting her mother to see her

disheveled appearance and to be horrified by the idea that she was going out with an attractive man in such a state.

If Hélène was upset, she tried not to show it. Juliet hadn't taken into account that—in front of handsome young men—no one's appearance was more important to Hélène than Hélène's. "D'accord," she said. "I won't expect you for dinner. Au revoir, Jim."

Poor Jim looked so confused by the exchange, but he managed a good-bye as Juliet practically dragged him outside.

"Take me to that out-of-the-way place we went the first day we met. With him."

Jim didn't ask questions and she didn't try to explain. She just put on the bike helmet and held fast to Jim's waist. This time, she didn't notice how his shoulders felt against her body. Her mind didn't wander at all. She willed all thoughts from her head and just clung to him, leaning into the curves and turns, trembling as the wind blew up into her helmet. Each strand of her hair pulled against her scalp. She closed her eyes and let the speed wash over her.

When they got to the cemetery, Juliet hopped off like she was an old pro, then reached into the sidecar and found the beers she'd known would be there. Popping the tops off two, she gave one to Jim and then drank what had to be half of her own in one gulp.

She didn't love the taste, but she did love the feeling of warmth that churned through her, making everything a little fuzzier.

"Will you tell me what's going on?" Jim said. He drank some

of his beer but was mostly looking at her as if he might have to restrain her.

"He's betraying me. He's seeing her," Juliet said, pacing back and forth in front of the tombstones.

"Who, Rosaline?" Jim said. And when Juliet whipped her head toward him, she could tell that he knew he'd made a mistake.

"How do you know about her?" Juliet said. "Did Romeo tell you? Is he proud? Do you admire him for having us both?" She stomped her boot into the ground as if daring Jim to lie to her.

Lifting both hands in the air in defense, Jim said, "No. She just showed up at this warehouse thing. He danced with her. He might have kissed her. Really, she kissed him."

"What? He kissed her, too?" She felt faint as her knees wobbled.

"It wasn't the way he kisses you," Jim said, looking past her into the sky. The clouds were blazes of orange and red, the dipping sun almost burning. "But he loves you. I talked to him about it. I believe him."

"Oh, you believe him. And he says he loves me," Juliet said, throwing her empty bottle so that it shattered against a small round headstone. "That's easy to say. And say and say and say. But maybe what he loves is having his secret cake and eating it, too."

"That saying has never made sense. Of course you eat the cake that you have," Jim said. "It's the whole point of cakes."

"Just . . . never mind," Juliet said. "I can't believe he kissed her." She kicked the toe of her boot into the base of a tombstone, sending a dusty chunk of dried mud to the ground.

"Kisses don't mean anything. He's doing it to protect you." Jim was behind her, with a hand on her shoulder.

She spun around. "Protect me from what? I never asked to be protected. I asked to be his love. I'd have risked things for him. Now I know why he never wanted to."

She pulled at her hair, almost wanting to rip it from her head. Jim was in front of her in two steps and grabbed her wrists, gently prying her fingers out from within the long strands. Now his face was close to her own. He had no traces of the familiar grin she'd grown used to.

"That's not it," he said. "He's right to want to protect you. You even told me how there are people who want to do you both harm and who want to see you fail. Aren't your companies both going to be bought?"

She scowled at him. Why did he have to be so calm and rational about this? And why was he bringing up their businesses? He sounded just like Romeo, and right now she wanted to hear nothing that sounded like Romeo.

Even though she liked the way his warm, strong hands felt around the cool skin of her wrists, she yanked her arms away. "What does that matter to anyone? How do we hurt anyone by being together?"

"I don't know, but everything is leverage," Jim said softly. "And it's easy to say it doesn't matter, but I know you don't want to hurt your family. Or lose them."

Ugh. Why did he have to be right?

She ignored Jim. She didn't want to talk about family.

She opened a fresh beer and took a sip so it made her body vibrate, then moved a step closer to Jim.

She was going to do what she wanted.

Looking for a long set of seconds at his eyes, his jaw, his lips, she said, "So if I kiss you, it means nothing?"

CHAPTER 24

JIM

"IT DOESN'T HAVE to mean anything. Sometimes a kiss is just a kiss," Jim said, knowing that was a lyric to some old song. But it was true, right? He backed up a little more as Juliet took another step closer. She'd blindsided him with that question, and he couldn't get his brain to work well enough to come up with an answer. Or at least, not the answer he knew he should give. "When Romeo and I box, I punch him and it's an exercise. It's not a feeling."

"A kiss is different from a punch," Juliet said. Her eyes were glistening with tears. Her hair was a mess from the ride over. She was thoughtful and unsmiling. She'd never been more beautiful.

Jim had to think, and stepped back, forcing his body to move away from her.

"He's kissed her, how many times now? They don't all mean nothing." She threw up her hands, as if to count to infinity.

"I'm telling you, they're no big deal," Jim said. He knew Juliet's train of thought wasn't purely on the Romeo and Rosaline track. He bit his own lip as if holding himself back. Of course he wanted to kiss Juliet. He'd wanted to since they'd met, since she'd held him tight as he steered them over the streets of Paris.

There. It was out now. He'd pulled that wish from the deep recesses of his brain, and the truth was at the forefront of his mind.

No, it was the only thought in his mind.

Yes, he wanted to kiss her.

But he wouldn't. She was Romeo's. This would work itself out.

They were all friends.

Young. Alive. Friends.

"Well, then if I kiss you, it should be no big deal." Juliet had him cornered. Behind him was a monument with a tall stone angel on its top. Its gray wings spread out over them both, to bless or to curse them, he didn't know.

He stepped to the left, fumbling his feet in the grass. She was the one who'd been drinking but he was the one who was clumsy. Drunk on the possibility of kissing her, nervous about what would happen if he did. He was already carrying around the worry of what he'd told his father about her and Romeo. Would another secret be so bad?

She reached him and, with her hand wrapped tight around his wrist, simultaneously pulled him to her as she pushed him toward a gravestone.

She pressed into him. She had one hand on his wrist and another on his shoulder, as if wanting to hold him in place.

He let his arms go around her. He let his face come close to hers, their cheeks brushing one another. He let himself feel the lightness and the density of her, knowing he could lift her up and carry her to the soft ground and press his lips to her.

The thought of kissing a woman for the first time had never consumed him this way. Usually, it was easy to do, a thoughtless reflex. He left behind wreckage and walked away unscathed.

But he wanted Juliet more than he had those other girls. In fact, everything about this situation was different.

And somehow, using more strength than he knew he had, he gently pushed her away. He didn't want to, not at all. He hated how much he wanted her and hated not knowing why he wanted her so much. Why did having her, or the idea of having her, mean so much to him? What did it prove or show that he hadn't proven or shown before with so many other women?

"You'll regret this," he said. "I'll regret this. You're sad. You're drunk. You're not thinking right."

Juliet looked up at him as though he'd betrayed her in every way possible.

But then she let go of him. "You're right," she said. "It's just Romeo. It's just me. It's just us."

She laughed sadly and stared off over the graveyard.

Jim didn't know what to say. That "just us" didn't include him, he sensed. Would it ever, really?

"I'll take you home."

CHAPTER 25

JULIET

TODAY WAS JULIET'S birthday. She was seventeen—almost an adult. She closed her eyes, thinking about the almost-adult mistake she'd made with Jim last week.

There'd been no further get-togethers with the three of them, or with just Romeo, but more due to school and circumstances than anything specific. And when she saw Jim and Romeo walking the halls together, she was almost grateful that Capulets and Montagues hated each other, as it gave her an excuse to avoid eye contact with both of them.

Now it was the weekend, and her day stretched out endlessly. She almost wished her father wasn't traveling, because that had thrown a wrench in the usual Capulet birthday celebration.

They would have a party or an outing for Juliet once he'd returned.

She hadn't yet heard from Romeo but knew he wouldn't forget. There'd been a note in their secret account early in the week asking what she'd like to do. She'd responded, *Surprise me.* She wanted desperately to see him and she also didn't. She wanted answers to all her questions.

Jim was one of those questions. The scene in the cemetery with Jim had been on a loop in her mind all week. How close they'd come and how far she'd known she would go.

She could pretend nothing happened, right? Nothing really did. Jim had seen to that.

But it didn't mean she wasn't still thinking about it. It didn't mean she was glad he had stopped them. Her imagination of the event had made it almost more real than if it had actually happened.

But she'd scrub it out of her mind.

The same way Lu Hai straightened her room, putting away the clothes Juliet left everywhere to make it seem like no damage had ever been done.

Her phone trilled, shattering any illusion in her neat room that her life was all in place.

Jim.

She answered. *"Allo?"*

Her voice was sharp and she knew it. Her tone, she thought, bore in it the instruction to not bring up the other thing.

"Hi. Look, I'm not calling to talk about us, or whatever. I mean, it is about us, but it's not. I mean, nothing happened." Jim was fumbling over his words in a way that made Juliet feel tender toward him. "But I keep thinking about it anyway. And I know I shouldn't."

Well, at least she hadn't made a total fool of herself if he was tormented by the memory, too.

"But you're both my friends," he said. "And, um, Romeo texted me. He said how it was your birthday and thought you might like if we all did something. I tried to say maybe just the two of you should do something. . . ."

"No, all three of us is good," Juliet said quickly. She didn't know if she wanted to be alone with Romeo, and she knew that was due to guilt. She couldn't avoid them both forever but thought her discomfort might be lessened with Jim present. At least she could divide her awkward feelings between the two of them.

"Okay, so we go out with Romeo and we act . . ."

"Normal?"

"Yes, normal," Jim agreed. "I'll call Romeo," he went on, and his voice soothed her even as it made her heart jump with nervousness. "And I'll pick you up, since, you know, I can. He thought we should go to that bar in the Petite Asie from the day I first met you both. That's fine, right?"

"Okay," Juliet said. She was relieved in a way to have him taking charge, but also a touch wounded that he seemed able to think so clearly and dispassionately about the whole thing.

He had told her it mattered, though. But if she'd really gotten under his skin, why was it so easy for him to basically hand her back to Romeo? He could have had her and he hadn't wanted her. God, did either of them?

And why was it so important to her? Her head told her to rise above all of it, to go and be the amazing woman she could become. But she could barely hear her head's rational lies over the truth that beat in her heart.

"I mean, unless . . . you don't want to," Jim said now. And in his voice she heard the same doubt and hope she couldn't suppress.

"No," she said, with more certainty than she felt. "No. Normal is good."

"Okay, I'll see you tonight," Jim said.

"Tonight."

Normal.

As if anything in her life had ever been normal.

CHAPTER 26

JIM

HE DIDN'T BRING her a birthday gift. He could have thought of a million beautiful objects not worthy of her, but they were just friends, and newish friends at that. He would buy her a drink and buy Romeo a drink and the world would be as it was.

He did, however, get off his bike and go to the door, like last week. But last week, he'd come as just her friend. Today was fraught with confusion.

He didn't have time to let his emotional cocktail take hold, because Lu Hai answered.

"Hi," he said, more intimidated by this woman than he was by any of Juliet's actual family members.

"You again," she said. "I open the door and here's Mr. America."

"Yeah, um, shouldn't you be with Juliet? I thought you were her nanny?"

Lu Hai shook her head like this was stupid. "Yeah, she's seventeen. What am I supposed to do? Stand around until she needs her tears wiped?"

Jim chuckled grimly, not wanting to think what could wring tears from Juliet at this point. "I'm, um, here to pick her up. For her birthday."

Lu Hai stood back from the door, letting Jim inside. Hélène crossed the foyer in front of him, stopping and raising an exquisitely groomed eyebrow.

"You're seeing each other very often, *non*?" she said.

"Well, I like coming to see you," Jim joked, knowing from Juliet's descriptions of her mother that Hélène would enjoy the compliment.

Hélène laughed and said, "You Americans have more charm than I'd been led to believe. And I didn't think boys your age would come to the door for a girl. I like that, even if I don't like your motorcycle."

"I'll be careful, I promise," Jim said, wondering how he could enjoy that he'd entertained Juliet's mother while at the same time hate himself for wanting so badly to impress her.

He and Juliet—even the potential for them—could never exist the way he wanted. He knew that Romeo loved her, and he'd come too close to betraying him.

When Juliet came downstairs, he couldn't help but notice how pretty she was—no, beyond pretty—like the kind of seventeen-year-old girl who made other seventeen-year-old girls fear they weren't doing this right. (Though the truly lovely thing about Juliet was that she'd never act like this was the case.)

"Maman, Jim is taking me out for my birthday. *C'est d'accord?*"

"Yes, just make sure you're not too late."

Even though they were out in the open air, he felt like they were boxed in on the bike. And was it just him or was Juliet's grip on his waist looser than it had been the other times they'd ridden together?

He parked in the back alley.

"Happy birthday to me," Juliet said forlornly as she walked into the bar just ahead of him. Jim hadn't brought up Romeo or Rosaline, hoping that she'd worked that out on her own. But what if that wasn't what was bothering her? Was it possible she was bothered by what had almost happened between them?

The bar was more crowded than it had been that first day when they met. It had seemed so long ago, but it had only been a bit more than a month. There was music playing over the craggy sound system and a band at the front, setting up.

They looked around for Romeo but he hadn't arrived. The bar's cheap drinks and proximity to so many hostels meant most of the patrons were their age or a few years older. If not for all the dread in his belly, Jim would have been looking forward to a really good time.

A cluster of girls with patched-up canvas backpacks danced in a circle. He could tell immediately they were Americans.

"They're pretty," Juliet said, following Jim's eyes from the bar to the girls. The shortest one was the most attractive, with a compact body and a long tangle of auburn hair.

"Yeah," Jim agreed, but without much enthusiasm. Juliet was standing so close to him he could smell her citrus perfume along with the smell of her, a smoky, soapy fragrance that made him want to bury his face in her neck and sleep there for a while.

But her expression was faraway. She looked toward the door without really looking, like an actress waiting to take the stage who's thinking of her lines as she gazes out over the heads of the audience.

Jim knew she'd have to give a performance. Even if they had stopped short of doing anything real that day at the cemetery, he and Juliet had a secret between them now.

The door near the front opened, letting in light from the street and illuminating Romeo's familiar lean frame. Jim's muscles tensed, like he was about to have a duel in an old Western. But Romeo wasn't there to duel. He was there so that Jim could lie to his face and pretend he wasn't in love with the love of Romeo's life.

Romeo waved at Juliet and Jim and strode toward them. The girls looked longingly at Romeo—probably because he was so clearly French and they'd probably decided one of them was going to hook up with a French guy tonight.

But Romeo didn't even notice them, he seemed so focused on

getting to Juliet. The smile on his face when he saw them was easy and happy.

Guilt gripped Jim even harder. He'd wanted Juliet so badly that day that he'd purposely put Romeo out of his head. Even that he'd blurted out knowing about Rosaline—had that been his subconscious attempt to drive her closer to him?

He knew it was.

At least he'd pushed her away.

"Hey, man," Jim said, fist-bumping Romeo while trying to come up with what to say next. "Need a drink?"

He wanted to buy Romeo a drink desperately. He needed something to do with his money, his hands, his eyes. But Romeo shook his head. "No rush," he said. "We have all night."

He pulled Juliet to him and kissed her. *"Bon anniversaire, mon amour."*

Jim watched Juliet's face for a hint of her reaction, but she just smiled and kissed Romeo back.

Like normal.

Jim hated her for a second. How could she?

He had to redirect this energy toward a new target.

The cute girl from the dance floor was coming toward the bar. Toward him.

Guess he had his target.

CHAPTER 27

ROMEO

JULIET HAD GONE to the bathroom. Again.

She was acting strange. A few times, Romeo caught her staring at Jim with concern. And when the little redhead came up to talk to Jim, had Juliet turned away to look at the television above the bar on purpose?

Maybe Romeo was just imagining it.

He had no idea what could be causing her to act so cagey. He flip-flopped between wanting to ask her and wanting to just get drunk and let things be.

Yeah, wasn't it better to leave it be?

He didn't know.

She came back from the bathroom, her hair tamed and her lips with a light coating of lipstick. Juliet almost never wore lipstick. She didn't need it, but it did enhance her beauty. She had on a soft black T-shirt big enough to fall from her left shoulder, exposing the creamy skin there. She'd cinched her waist with a patchwork scarf and wore a worn-in pair of Levi's and black motorcycle boots.

When she reached them, Romeo pulled her to him. "Get us some drinks, would you?" he asked Jim.

"Yeah, of course, bro," Jim said.

"'Bro'?" Romeo wrinkled his brow at his friend. When someone felt like your brother, the term *bro* seemed to feel like it wasn't enough. And it certainly wasn't a very Jim thing to say.

But he let it go and turned to Juliet, taking her hands in his. Her grip on his hands was loose. He squeezed her small palms, hoping for her to return the gesture. He loved the way she held tight no matter what.

When she didn't squeeze back, he pulled her to him for a kiss. A kiss she accepted but returned with only the slightest of pressure. "Someone will see," she said by way of explanation, and looked around the crowded bar as if to prove it.

Maybe she'd just now started to take him seriously, about protecting them. But he was trying to play things her way and not control everything.

He handed her a small box. If he gave her the gift and she was still being strange, then he'd ask what was going on.

"Bon anniversaire," he said.

Juliet took the box from him and glanced up with a strange expression. "I thought we said . . ."

"We did," Romeo allowed. When they'd met, they'd agreed their secret would be safer if they gave no gifts, but it was her birthday and he felt compelled to. Not out of any guilt or duty but just because. "Just because" being the best reason to give any gift. "But I wanted to," he told her.

She looked into his eyes with curiosity, and he wondered what she expected to see there. He wondered if her feelings of suspicion had been aroused again because of their time apart. But he hadn't seen Rosaline since the warehouse party. How did people actually cheat on people they loved when it was this hard carrying around guilt for what was essentially nothing?

"Open it," he said, pointing to the little box.

Juliet bent her head over the package and unwrapped it with great care, peeling back each piece of tape and pulling aside the wrapping paper like whatever was beneath might break if she touched it wrong. Romeo watched in suspense, wanting her to love it.

Inside was a gold necklace with a tiny vial at the end. "Open the vial," he instructed her.

She unscrewed the tiny cap and pulled out the miniature scroll inside. It read, *A.V.O. Ours most of all.*

Jim returned with drinks before Juliet could react. Or did she not want to react?

"Do you like it?" Romeo asked. Was it jerky of him to have expected her to seem more grateful?

"Yes," she said, and now he saw that maybe there was a tear in her eye. "I love it. Help me put it on."

"What is going on?" Romeo whispered into her hair as he fastened the necklace around her slender neck. "I thought you'd be more excited."

"Nothing, I love it," Juliet said, reaching back to squeeze his hand. "It's just how crowded this place is. See, we have company."

The redhead who'd chatted up Jim earlier had come back with him now. She came up to his shoulder and she leaned on him as if they'd been a couple for years. She was definitely American. "You look so familiar," she was saying to him.

Jim smiled and took a sip of his beer. He rolled his eyes at Romeo, as if this kind of drunken recognition was a trick women used on him all the time. For all Romeo knew, it probably was.

"I get that a lot," he said. "I think it's just my face."

"No, no, isn't this you?" the girl said, walking to the edge of the bar and picking up a newspaper that was strewn across the surface. Places like this opened early enough that big-time drunks could sip their morning bourbon while reading *Figaro*.

Romeo could see Jim's face grow pale, even in the dim light of the bar. He was shaking his head with such vigorous denial that Romeo had to find out what this was all about.

Romeo pulled the paper from the hands of the stunned American.

It was Jim, with James Redmond. Eating dinner. In the Eiffel Tower.

The caption read, "A Family Affair."

Romeo's teeth pressed against each other as he tried to read the accompanying story. He could barely get through it as blood flowed to his clenched fists. What he could digest mentioned the proposed takeover of the Houses of Montague and Capulet. Jim Gardner was Jim Redmond, son of James Redmond, who was planning to buy the two houses and slice, dice, and merge them into some streamlined shell of their former selves. Romeo didn't have to read any more.

"What is this?" Romeo said, shoving the paper into Jim's chest. "What is this? This is your father?" His voice was shaky but loud. He pushed his weight against Jim, sending Jim back a few steps. But Jim's hands were in the air, like a surrender. It infuriated Romeo even more. He wanted a reason to crush the American scum, but he wasn't going to throw a punch at someone who might not fight back.

He crumpled the paper and threw it down with all the force he wanted to use on Jim. Juliet grabbed it from the floor and opened it, then looked up with tears in her eyes.

She emitted a soft, heartbroken cry. "How could you? How could you do this to me?" she said to Jim. It wasn't just that she'd said "to me" and not "to us," but something worse in her tone that crept along Romeo's bones like an ugly, prickly vine. She sounded like Jim had betrayed *her*, not *them*.

Jim looked from Romeo to Juliet and didn't say anything at first. He still looked stunned, like his secret was just being revealed to him instead of the other way around.

The redhead backed away. "Oh-kay," she said. "I guess I shouldn't have pressed the subject."

Romeo's fists still vibrated with an urge to punch Jim. He

should have. But the guy didn't even deserve a real fight. It wouldn't hurt him enough. What would? He was a traitor. He was a liar. He was never the friend Romeo had believed he was.

And Juliet was standing too far away. She should have been next to him, leveling Jim with a glare that buttressed all his anger. Romeo tried to control it, but he felt his arm draw back and he punched Jim in the face. There was no love in it this time. He felt cold satisfaction as Jim's body sprawled against the bar, as his hand flew to his eye, which was already darkening.

The American girl who'd shown them the paper shrieked and scurried to join her friends.

"It's not like you think," Jim said, struggling back to his feet. "I didn't do anything." His hands remained up in an "I'm innocent" pose. His jaw was trembling. His normally cocky gaze was replaced by a humbled, saddened look of being lost. But Romeo didn't feel sorry for him. He was just a worthless American liar, and who knew how else he'd fucked them over?

Now Juliet spoke.

"But you didn't say that James Redmond was your father," she said. "Why would you keep that a secret?"

"I don't have a good answer for that," Jim told them. His eyes were focused somewhere on the space between them, rather than actually at either Romeo or Juliet. Romeo wondered if the asshole actually felt bad or was just avoiding their eyes because he thought they were so far beneath him for not figuring it out sooner.

"This was just a game to you," Romeo said, and now he closed in on Jim, pushing him a little so Jim's back hit the bar. Who cared if he wasn't ready for it? Romeo didn't care about being the bigger man. He just wanted to hurt this guy. "I suppose we're part of the hostile takeover."

Jim didn't say anything. To Romeo, it was silence that admitted everything. To think he'd thought of Jim as a brother.

"Juliet, let's go," he said, pulling her toward the door.

But Juliet drew her arm away. She did it just slowly enough that he could literally feel her slipping away from him.

"No," she said. "I'm not being hauled off like some prize. I can be mad of my own accord."

She looked from Romeo to Jim and then back.

And she was the first to leave.

CHAPTER 28

JIM

HE WAS ALONE.

Again.

Juliet had left.

Then Romeo.

He wasn't someone well versed in apologizing. Besides, he wasn't sure an apology was what he needed to do. Maybe this was just who he was.

His father did hostile takeovers.

And Jim made friends and screwed them over.

What was the point anymore of even trying?

"We've let you ruin enough," Romeo had said.

And he hadn't even known the half of it.

Without speaking, the bartender slid a glass of ice to him. Jim pressed it to his eye and ordered another drink, feeling and looking every bit the Ugly American.

CHAPTER 29

JULIET

JULIET WOKE IN a fog the next day. The covers were over her head and she breathed the thick heat of her sleep, sure that there was no better place for her than bed.

She didn't want to see Jim or Romeo. She didn't want to be with anyone.

Not with Jim. She didn't trust him.

Not with Romeo. She didn't believe him.

Not with herself. Today, more than ever, she really wished she were someone else.

"Juliet. Juliet." A hand was shaking her out of bed. Her father. Why was her father in her room? She pulled back the top corner of her covers, putting her palm over the necklace Romeo had given her, trying to hide it.

Was this about Romeo? Her father knew, didn't he? Jim had told. Why would Jim tell? To break them up. Or maybe something crueler.

These thoughts careered inside her and she sprang up from the bed, about to tell her father everything.

She looked up into his eyes, expecting to see disappointment, anger . . . but not what she saw. Panic and fear shot out from his dilated pupils.

"It's Henri," he said. His normally booming voice was wispy even though his grip on her arm was tight. "He's dead."

In the week that followed, she felt like she never left her bed. She did, of course. She had to, as preparations were made and flowers arrived and her mother cried and her father swore and Lu Hai silently maintained the order of Juliet's room, even as disorder spiraled around them.

There were messages in the secret email account from Romeo. She didn't reply. Jim called her. She didn't answer. Emails and phone calls flooded her—from Gabrielle, Catrine, Margaux. She felt at liberty to ignore everything.

She wandered the house like she was the ghost, and continued to breathe the same air she'd breathed before she learned Henri was dead.

Her brother had been murdered. That's what they were saying, anyway. A maid had found his body in one of those apartments in the Ninth. Or, what appeared to be his body. He'd been badly burned. His teeth had been removed, indicating foul play. A test on the remains found his DNA, and unsinged was his Capulet signet ring.

Juliet twisted her own ring, thinking of the awful visit to the De Molay Hospital in the Marais. The family had been summoned to the morgue before the official autopsy, but the whole thing seemed like a special kind of torture. There was no body to be seen. Just a brisk nurse handing them a bag with the scorched ring. Nothing else in the apartment was burned, indicating he'd been killed in another location and brought there.

Now, Juliet was in the back of a hearse.

Numb.

She knew she was supposed to cry. She wanted to cry. She wanted the release of it; she wanted tears because they'd make her feel emptied.

Instead, she felt a nothingness so solid she thought she might turn to stone.

Was this her comeuppance for doing whatever she wanted?

If she hadn't been so entangled with Romeo and with Jim, would Henri still be alive?

She thought back to that last conversation they'd had and scoured it for hints. She thought now that he had wanted to tell her something that day, but she'd been so eager for revenge on Romeo that she'd missed it.

And now her brother was gone. Who knew what he'd been

thinking as he died? Who would want to kill him like they had?

People were looking into it. The family had been assured the killers would be brought to justice. Juliet thought these were more lies.

All she could do now was watch her brother be put into the ground.

The cemetery was much nicer than the one Jim had taken her and Romeo to. Père Lachaise was the resting place of Oscar Wilde, the writer; Jim Morrison, the rock star; and Maria Callas, the opera singer. Being so filled with "names" meant only people who had the money could bury their dead here now. The smallest plot cost thirteen thousand euros. But the Capulets had a mausoleum—a circular, marble-walled fortress with a cluster of sculpted angels looming above it. The inside held a set of damp passageways that curved and wended along walls that housed the entombed Capulets.

Neither of her parents cared about what the thing cost or if it was the best. Like Juliet, Hélène and Maurice had gone rigid. It was the Capulet way, to show nothing of what they were truly feeling. Her mother, she knew, would just go deeper into the superficial after this—try to make her life pretty and light to hide all the hurt she'd lived. And her father would do his best to be strong, because too much questioning would make him wonder if it was his fault his son was dead.

The church service had been small, just the immediate family and servants who'd known Henri since childhood. Her parents, betraying their unspoken vows of showing only strength, had wept openly during the sermon, but Juliet could only stand between them, holding their hands, feeling uncertain whether she was holding them up or the other way around.

In the limo, Juliet allowed her father to stare sadly at the passing scenery. He didn't worry her as much as her mother did, because Maurice would have things he had to do. But her mother would keep retreating into herself, covering her misery so that things could still seem perfect. Saddened by the thought, Juliet cuddled close to her mother, as she had when she was a young girl. She felt relief when her mother's cool hand petted the hair out of her eyes.

"Will it be okay, Maman?" Juliet whispered.

Her mother clutched Juliet's shoulder and pressed her lips against her daughter's temple. "No, but we will do our best," Hélène said, and Juliet felt the slightest bit heartened by this little truth as they pulled onto the narrow path that led to the mausoleum where Henri would be interred.

As she stepped out of the limo, Juliet saw a crowd had already gathered, awaiting the family procession to the gravesite. Shareholders, actors, lawyers, models, businesspeople. All of them in their best black, some of them vying to be the most photoworthy at the funeral.

And for every person, there seemed to be three paparazzi, pushing their way in. They forced themselves through the crowds to get shots of the Capulets. As much as Juliet loathed them, though, they at least were working. It sickened her even more to see the preening poses of the funeral-goers around her, hopeful that if they were going to be in a shot, they'd look glamorous.

"Did any of you even know Henri?" Juliet muttered under her breath as she walked down the passageway left by the onlookers.

Surprisingly, Hélène didn't scold her, only squeezed her arm lightly to calm her. "*Je sais*, Juliet. Just be strong." Her voice wavered.

Gabrielle, wearing a sedate dress that did nothing for her million-dollar figure, came up alongside Juliet and put an arm around her. "I'm so sorry," she said sincerely, with none of her trademark Gabrielle jocularity. "I loved him," she added, more to herself, the candor unlike her. Juliet knew she was being honest.

But many others, Juliet thought, seemed to think the funeral was a party. Catrine and Margaux wore exotic feathered veils and were eyeballing the male models in attendance. One of the shareholders, a commercial real estate developer, slipped his card to the head of the bank that oversaw the family trust.

"This is disgusting," Juliet said to Gabrielle. Over Gabrielle's shoulder, Juliet caught Thibeau and Pierre (were they really friends now?) glad-handing with some Capulet board members, like this was a cocktail party that just happened in the cemetery. She hoped one day that each of their worlds would collapse so that she could treat their situations with the same jovial opportunism.

"I know, and I'm not even a good person," Gabrielle agreed. "At least they're here and not at the Montagues' thing."

"The Montagues' thing?" Juliet's heart alternately fluttered and cringed at the name.

"Yeah, while you're putting your brother underground, they're having a party on a yacht," Gabrielle said. "Can you say horrible?"

"What do you mean?" Juliet strained to make sense of what Gabrielle was telling her. Her brother, her father's son, was dead—had been *murdered*—and the Montagues were on a boat? Having a party?

She dug her fingernails into her palms until it seemed she might draw blood.

She had arrived at the gravesite without even noticing. White lilies surrounded the entry to the mausoleum, waiting to accept what was left of her brother—an almost-empty mahogany box. He was more gone from her life than she ever imagined he could be. She'd been fighting to keep him from exile, never daring to imagine something like this could happen.

Cry, she thought. *Cry*. Tears would drain her, maybe even shatter her, and she wanted that.

But nothing would come. The sky sank with the weight of heavy clouds. The clouds would cry before she did.

She was all she had now. Henri was gone. Jim was gone. Romeo was gone.

No, Romeo wasn't gone.

Romeo was cold and callous and on a boat, celebrating what? That the people he cared about were still alive?

He was dead to her.

Her eyes saw nothing and her ears heard nothing and her skin was cold to the touch; she might as well have been made of steel.

Juliet reached for her mother's hand and squeezed it. Hélène's hand felt like death itself, but she squeezed back faintly as the priest continued to talk over the muffled sobs of mourners.

"Some things are not meant for this earth. Some people cannot be ours, no matter how much we want to keep them."

Juliet thought he was talking about more than Henri.

But she still couldn't cry.

CHAPTER 30

ROMEO

HE SHOULD HAVE been with her.

Her brother was dead.

The Capulets were at a funeral. And he was on a boat.

"I hope you don't have plans today, Romeo." His mother had caught him just as he was headed out the door, restless and wanting to figure out how to get a message to Juliet. He'd left an email in their secret account and gotten no reply—he didn't blame her— and he didn't think he should text her, either. He'd barely slept the night after the argument at the bar—trying to figure out what to do and how to handle Jim and his treachery. Before he could do anything, though, the news had come about Juliet's brother. She'd hate Romeo if he expressed any worry over something as relatively inconsequential as them being discovered, or even about Jim and his betrayal.

Everything had become that much worse. He didn't know Henri, but he knew Juliet loved her brother, and that was enough. He could only imagine how awful she felt. She needed him more than ever and he couldn't help her.

He looked at his mother's pretty, impassive face. "I did. Why?"

"We've rented a yacht, for a party. A House of Montague special event. You're needed." She tapped the screen of her phone. "Invite Benoit. Invite your other friends. Girls. Pretty ones."

If it had been his father asking, he might have argued. But his mother, with her jade eyes on the verge of disappointment, was someone he couldn't turn down.

"And what does this have to do with me?" He asked it not with petulance but with genuine curiosity. The House of Montague had special events all the time. His presence was rarely so coveted.

"Youth is good for business, my love," his mother said, surveying her nails and then tapping her phone to send a text to the manicurist who visited the house. Catherine Montague was very tech-savvy. "If your father and I invite our friends, it's just the middle-aged rich on a yacht. If we send you out with the prettiest models, it's gossip and relevance for the brand. You know that. And how many mothers would demand their sons go drink champagne with models?"

Romeo raised an eyebrow. "Isn't it bad form to do it on the day that Henri Capulet is being buried?"

Catherine looked at him like she was surprised he knew who Henri was, much less cared. "That is a shame, about that Capulet boy. But all the more reason to be in the press: Death has a certain glamour, and that family will be all over the news."

"Wow, way to be charitable," Romeo said, but under his breath. Catherine wasn't paying attention, as she'd gone back to making her appointments.

"Yes, you're a lucky boy," Catherine said, responding to something Romeo hadn't said.

Romeo knew it was true—he was lucky—but part of him wished for a life where he and his girlfriend could be people who'd never set foot on a yacht, much less ones who did it to make headlines.

I don't want this life, he thought to himself.

(A smaller voice in the back of his head asked him, *But is that true, Romeo?*)

Benny was drunk before they even reached the Pont Henri IV—how tacky was it that the launch bore the dead Capulet's name?—on the right bank of the Seine. The Montague town car's stash of whiskey always called to Benny, and Romeo didn't have the energy to tell his cousin it was kind of idiotic to board a boat already wasted. Romeo couldn't even remember the last party his cousin had arrived at sober, but what was he, Benny's AA sponsor?

Besides, his mind was on Juliet. He'd covertly checked the news on the way over and had seen that she'd be getting to the funeral right about now.

He'd called on a few friends from school but had left most of the guest list to his mother's behind-the-scenes PR orchestrating. If it had been last week, he would have invited Jim. What kind of disaster would that be? He still couldn't believe he'd been stupid enough to trust him. He'd wanted to blame Juliet for ever letting them go with Jim in the first place but Romeo eventually decided the Jim thing was his own fault. All the trouble he took to hide his and Juliet's relationship and then he let them get on a motor-cycle with a stranger.

He'd left a message in the drafts folder yet again to say something about Henri, but he'd gotten no response. And could he blame her? He'd debated sending secret flowers and contemplated how he might get a message to her, but nothing seemed right.

Everything was broken. What idiot let the love of his life suffer alone while he was on a yacht with social climbers and celebrities?

He felt caged already, a feeling made worse because he knew Rosaline was here and he'd be forced to act like they were something to each other. He wanted to run from the dock. A sense of duty bound him. The sense was made even deeper by the fact that he felt like he'd screwed up with Jim. He had to be on this boat and do what his family needed.

The yacht, a luxury boat frequently chartered for private parties of the very rich, was already teeming with models, actors and actresses, and the most up-and-coming of up-and-coming French pop stars and hip-hop artists. The boarding music, though, was a chill Air track that bubbled over the proceedings the same way the pink champagne already overflowed from glasses.

Romeo didn't even like champagne, but he took two glasses from a passing waiter and downed them. The feeling he hated, that warm burn in his chest, didn't matter. He took two more.

Why did he have to be so careful to be the good son?

He drank down the next two. His legs felt loose and uncertain and the boat hadn't even moved.

The day was warm and the models were clad in bikinis and sheer cover-ups that only served to draw attention to their curves as the sun blazed through them. An attendant had just thrust another glass of champagne at Romeo when Rosaline catwalked up on her totally yacht-inappropriate sandals.

"*Bonjour*, sexy," she said, kissing his cheek. It felt so wrong that he almost backed away.

"Hi," he said. "I have to go say hello to some people." He didn't want to talk to her. His indifference, however, only made him feel even more that Rosaline was watching him as he went.

Benny was already in a circle of guys and models. At the center, two dancers who'd toured with DJ Kash were tangled together, swiveling their hips and swirling their long, thin arms in the air like they were casting a magic spell.

In a way, they were, because the guys watching were mesmerized. Benny looked at Romeo and said, "We're so lucky, man."

Lucky. That word again. He didn't feel it. He downed another champagne in one gulp and smiled at his friend.

But he hated him at that moment.

He hated everything he knew, except Juliet.

The yacht left the dock and he wanted to puke over the side.

He couldn't look at the water.

His family wanted him to have a good time. What was wrong with them? Even if they hated the Capulets, wasn't it a sign of pure evil to live it up when the Capulet family was mourning the death of a loved one?

Romeo wanted this over with. The best way to get it done was to lose himself in a blur of alcohol. Not thinking was better than thinking too much.

Photographers were everywhere—after all, that was the point.

Romeo glad-handed them all. He bombed every photo.

He tore off his shirt.

He danced in a throng of models, showing off terrible dance moves that made no sense to his limbs.

He jumped around with Benny and the guys when a particularly raucous rap song came on. He screamed at the top of his lungs.

He nearly got in a fight with Michel DeRolu, an actor who was in a French remake of *The French Connection*. But he fell on his face trying to throw the first punch.

He acted, in short, like an asshole.

He hoped this was good for the brand.

Two hours in, he was hurling over the railing of the ship as they passed Notre-Dame. Even drunk, he couldn't help but think of Juliet and that day they'd met Jim. He was trying to decide how he'd see her again. He was imagining what the world would be like if he could just be with her the way he wished he could.

Rosaline tottered up beside him just as the ship approached

the Île Saint-Louis Bridge. Her eye makeup was smeared as if she'd been crying, and she was clearly very intoxicated.

They matched. He wondered if his mother would like that.

He turned to her, putting a hand on her arm to steady her. "Rosaline," he said. He was as physically wrecked as she was, and they both leaned against the railing.

"Why are you avoiding me?" she asked, pressing into him with the full weight of her body. Romeo had to put a hand on her waist just to keep her from falling over. Or himself. He wasn't sure anymore.

The remnants of the puke in his mouth tasted awful.

"I'm not," he said. "I have to circulate. It's my party."

"But I want to be with you," Rosaline whined. Her breath was sour, like she might have thrown up, too.

"You are," he slurred, letting her wrap her arms around his neck like they were slow-dancing.

Rosaline's waifish figure was heavy against him and he continued to steady her with a hand on her waist.

"Look, I have to tell you something," he said, emboldened by his drinks and the fact that everything felt wrong today, so why not throw caution to the wind? "I can't be with you. I love someone else. And it's hard. And we can't be together. But I needed to tell you."

He was almost crying. He felt like shit on every level and now he was explaining himself to someone who only cared about herself.

But Rosaline seemed to gain clarity as the words made their

way to her perfect ears. Her eyes widened as she looked up at him, and her gaze was actually sweet, not angry. "You poor thing," she said, with real sympathy. "It explains so much. I just wish you had told me sooner. You should go to her."

He'd expected a slap, or yelling. Drunken, jealous anger.

She'd surprised him.

He loved her in that moment, for understanding and for being right.

It was the perfect photo op.

(Really, you'd think they were in love.)

If only the person who said pictures don't lie could have been inside Romeo's head, they'd have gotten the rest of the story. . . .

CHAPTER 31

JULIET

"I'D LIKE TO stay a bit," Juliet said to her parents as the last of the cars left the cemetery.

Her voice wasn't hers. It belonged to some sophisticated, jaded actress, someone who'd seen more and done more than Juliet and who'd know what mistake to make next.

It was the voice of someone playing the part of Juliet.

She expected her mother to argue. Leave her daughter in a graveyard? After what had happened to Henri, especially?

But her mother's eyes were faraway, glassy. Juliet suspected something chemical had whisked Hélène from reality. And her father could barely look at her, probably because he was fighting tears. She knew they were so consumed by grief, so numb, that they might let her do anything at this point. She could almost be hurt by the fact that they weren't worried she would get killed.

Could she hope for such a reprieve? Death seemed to her almost better than the tears she craved.

"We'll send a car for you when you're ready."

As the limo pulled away, the sky grew darker and the silence of the cemetery flowed over her.

She walked away from the mausoleum and sat down on a grave, still bare of grass. The dirt was soft beneath her and she stretched her legs along the top of the plot. There had to be some symbolism to sitting on a freshly made grave, but she didn't think she needed to go that deep.

She just wanted to die.

CHAPTER 32

JIM

JULIET'S BROTHER.

He'd liked him.

And he was dead.

Murdered, they were saying.

The grisly news was everywhere, as were people speculating over what had happened, who would want to kill Henri Capulet, and whether this was a trick and he was still alive. Most of the theories suggested a drug problem and an angry dealer and that, yes, he was indeed dead.

The family had not been reached for comment. The House of Capulet hadn't even released an official statement. It made sense to Jim. What did you say? "Our son is dead; business will go on as usual"? Because that was the truth, really, for all these rich families, but who wanted to admit it?

And what should he do in this situation? What did you do when the girl of your dreams, who no longer trusted you, whose boyfriend (or was he her ex now?) wanted to kill you, who was a target of your father's, now was at her brother's funeral?

Jim opened a beer and slouched on the couch, watching the news. Juliet at the funeral. He couldn't see her eyes beneath her wide-brimmed hat as she bent her head, but her lips were set in a tight line. He'd never had a sibling, so he had no idea what she could be feeling, but he knew from experience that she was capable of some powerful emotions.

He had to stop thinking about that night.

"Henri Capulet, he was pretty hot," Jennifer said, shaking him out of his thoughts about the almost-kiss. She sat down next to him, tapping away on her iPhone, like she hadn't just commented on the hotness of a dead guy. Her hair was damp and she was in her weekend clothing, jeans and a tight white T-shirt. She'd been at the house more and more.

"What's this?" His dad came out of the bedroom. He was freshly showered. Jim had the feeling that there'd been a non-business transaction between him and Jennifer.

"Oh, well, look at that," James said, with a glance at the TV. "Timing's perfect."

"I know," Jennifer said. "I'm sending those financials over to our people in the States. You know what they say. R.I.P. and thanks for the family secrets."

What were Jennifer and his father saying? Maybe Jim watched too many movies, but it sure seemed like they were talking about Henri. . . . What secrets? And what did "timing's perfect" mean? If Jim was really part of the family business, why hadn't he been told about this?

Jennifer tapped his shoulder. "Let's not watch this," she said. "Can you put on Bravo?"

He was riding his motorcycle to the cemetery he'd seen on TV when it began to rain. Maybe she'd still be there. Maybe she wouldn't.

Probably better for everyone if she wasn't.

But he still hoped she was.

CHAPTER 33

ROMEO

HE WAS GOING to her house.

He didn't care.

He was going to see her.

The Capulet family would open the door to find him, Romeo Montague, enemy combatant, archrival heir, and the man who loved their daughter.

Since they'd become a couple, he'd always taken pains not to walk by her house, even when he needed to go that way. They were only a few blocks apart on the same street, but he feared being seen, or giving something away just by the way he stepped on the sidewalk in front of the Capulets' door.

The rain was drenching everyone as they came off the yacht.

Models were shrieking like banshees who would melt if the water touched them.

He was wobbly and feeling nauseous from the champagne and the boat ride, but he only cared about seeing Juliet.

Benny called him. "Car's here," he said, standing next to the black sedan that had pulled up next to the dock to meet them.

Romeo shook his head. "Nope, I'm gonna walk," he told Benny.

"Are you nuts?"

Romeo ignored him and set out. The rain wasn't going to stop. It was beyond rain that rated a little extra coverage on the news. It was some kind of ancient rain. God-sending-a-message rain. Get-to-your-true-love-now-or-the-world-will-drown rain.

That he'd left his jacket at home was inconsequential. He needed to be soaked. He needed to suffer. His black shirt grew blacker as the downpour coursed over him.

He would suffer gladly, because once he reached her, he'd suffer no more. *They* would suffer no more.

God, he was drunk.

He tried to walk faster, but he was slipping on the sidewalk. Water ran into his shoes. Farther up the Seine, he spotted a guy climbing on a moped. Romeo ran for him.

Romeo pulled out his wallet. It was fat with cash. He still hadn't had time to ask someone to fix the issue with his credit card from the night at the warehouse party, so he'd withdrawn two thousand euros from the bank. Most of that was still in his wallet. It was idiotic, carrying it around, but he hadn't had the energy to be anything more than an idiot this week. At least now he was an idiot with a destination.

Waving his wallet, he hollered through the rain at the moped owner. "I'll give you all the cash I have in here for your bike."

Even in the rain, he could see the guy's facial expression turn incredulous, then fearful. But then, as Romeo drew closer, he could see on the biker's face—even through the blur of rain—sudden recognition that it was Romeo Montague about to buy his crappy-ass moped.

To show he meant business, Romeo extracted the wad of cash and started running toward the guy. He needed the bike and he needed it now.

"It's yours," the guy said, taking the cash and giving him the key. "Why would you even want it?"

But Romeo was already speeding away.

CHAPTER 34

JIM

SHE WAS THERE.

The rest of the funeral had left but she was still there, rain beating into her coat, her hair soaked, her hat from TV gone. Her face was turned upward, her fair profile statue-still against the steel gray of the sky.

It was so fucking wet outside that on the way over Jim hadn't even seen the vendors who sold umbrellas to tourists. The rain was that violent. He didn't know if he believed in God or anything, except when the weather did things like this. The rain the night his mom had hung herself was just like this.

He always thought of it as killer rain, rain to die by. And Juliet looked like she was glad to be its victim.

She looked like someone hoping to be struck by lightning, or crushed by something falling from the sky.

She looked like someone who wanted to die.

Jim knew that look.

He'd worn it and he'd seen it. And when she looked up at him with those death-filled eyes, it felt like home.

He reached for her. . . .

CHAPTER 35

ROMEO

HE WAS A man possessed.

He was flooring the piece-of-crap moped, barely able to see his own hands in front of him, much less the road.

The stupid bike wobbled and jerked and skidded. A single raindrop could have probably knocked it over, and Romeo was fending off a storm that pummeled him with sheets of water as if he were a puny target for a nasty hunter.

He wasn't like this. He always took time to think beforehand, to determine his course of action and make a beautiful gesture.

Riding over there on a bike that barely ran, soaked through, drunk, angry, crazed . . .

Nope, nothing beautiful about this gesture.

But the only person whose opinion mattered wouldn't care if he was a mess.

He sped through a red light, seeking heaven. But daring hell to claim him first.

THERE'S AN ALLEY in the Marais, just off the Rue du Temple, just out of the lamplight, just beyond the reveling throngs. It's where couples go to feel those ghosts of Paris past. It's the place for when they want to be scared just enough to fall deeper into one another's arms.

In the streaming rain, there is no one.

Just water, running down the cobblestoned gutters. So much water right now that you have to wonder, if they fill up enough, would it call forth something ancient and powerful?

Or is the rain just the right cover for the lone figure walking toward a door carved by hands that died centuries ago?

What business is so important that someone is visiting the

Knights Templar at this hour? In this weather? Did James Redmond's right-hand woman suddenly have an interest in ancient artifacts, or had she developed some deep religious fervor? The Templars were known for their deep ties in those areas.

Or was it their deep pockets Ms. Reynolds was looking to access? After all, art and religion wouldn't be what they are without money and power, and the Knights Templar certainly had plenty of both. They'd funded some of the best and worst pages in history, if you want to know the truth.

So, of course Jennifer Reynolds could bear a little rain when what the Templars control has seen others brave hellfire, damnation, and certain ruin.

The footfalls are soft but hurried. The umbrella serves to put the stranger inside a capsule of running water.

The figure stops at the door.

Extends a young hand.

Knocks three times.

Folds the umbrella.

Bows her blond head.

Steps inside.

Jennifer Reynolds.

American assistant to one James Redmond.

Not seeking shelter from the rain but walking in like she owns the place.

Or knows the owners very, very well.

CHAPTER 36

ROMEO

THE CAPULET HOUSE was lit from within and—even though there'd been a death—it was clear life was inside.

Several catering trucks lined the curb, workers in windbreakers ducking in a side door with trays of food. Mourners took fast steps from their cars to the front door, and slipped inside and out of the rain, folding up umbrellas as they did so.

Anything he, Romeo Montague, did here today would make a scene.

Sober, sane Romeo would never have shown up here on a day like today.

But today, he was neither sober nor sane.

They'd never let him in the front door. They'd buried their son. The face of the enemy wouldn't be welcome.

But he didn't want the front door anyway. He wanted to see Juliet on her balcony, like she'd talked about. She'd once revealed she longed for him to find her there, and call to her.

He'd always said how crazy that would be.

From now on, he'd give her anything she wanted. He'd run away with her if that's what it took. Nothing seemed crazy now.

But what if she wasn't up there? She could have been down-stairs with her family. He only wanted to see her. They could escape tonight if they wanted.

He texted her phone: *Come to your balcony. I need to see you. A.V.O.*

He didn't wait for an answer.

He dropped the moped by the curb, not caring that it clattered against the ground as if to announce a drunk idiot was outside.

Running through puddles, so soaking wet that he was sure he'd never dry, he slipped down the side street where he knew Juliet's balcony was.

There was almost no light in her room, but she would come. He knew she'd come. She probably hated being down there with the funeral-goers. He could only imagine how sad she must be. He'd do whatever he could to make it better.

"Juliet," he called, slipping in the muddy flower beds, falling to his knees and pulling himself back up. The mud was heavy and cold on his clothes. He was still wobbly from all the drinking and the horrible ride here. "Juliet," he tried again, louder this time. He couldn't even hear himself over the rain.

"Juliet!" he screamed raggedly up at the balcony. "Juliet! I need to see you!"

He saw figures in the rain, coming toward him. Big figures. Security? He didn't know or care.

Where was she?

He looked up at the balcony. He just needed to get up there. He'd break in if he had to.

A tree, shiny with rain, glistened next to the balcony. The branches rasped against the brick house as the wind pelted rain horizontally across the atmosphere.

"Hey," one of the figures called. Romeo couldn't see through the rain, which kept growing worse.

He'd climb the tree, up to her balcony.

If that didn't prove he'd do anything for her, nothing would.

CHAPTER 37

JULIET

SHE HEARD FOOTSTEPS behind her.

She looked grimly at the sky, her teeth chattering and her cheeks half frozen as the cold rain continued its assault.

Maybe someone was coming to kill her, as they had Henri.

Maybe she'd let them.

What did she have to lose anymore?

A hand grabbed her shoulder. She didn't flinch.

She turned and there in black was Jim. The Grim Reaper of something. Maybe the part of her she wished dead.

He opened his mouth to speak.

She didn't want to hear anything.

She stood, rainwater dripping from the hem of her skirt, her hair wet against her cheeks.

She grabbed him.

She pushed him against a stone, water rushing down the engraved name on its front.

She pressed her lips to his, hungry and wanting to obliterate him, obliterate everything.

They sank down into the mud, clutching each other. Maybe they'd be absorbed by the earth. Or maybe they'd be washed away, right off the face of it.

"Does it mean nothing?" she murmured into his open mouth.

He didn't answer.

Because she already knew.

He instantly gave himself up to her, like he'd been fighting his body's wants and then, with her lips on his, had relented.

He clutched her to him greedily and lifted her off the ground. She wrapped her legs around him.

Jim peeled her sodden blouse down, kissing her shoulders, breathing her in.

"Are you sure?" Jim said, but he was still holding her tightly against him, still sighing heavily as she put her lips to his neck, just below his ear.

"Yes," she said. That throaty, deep voice, like she was drunk on shadows. Like she wasn't herself. Like she couldn't find herself even if she tried.

Right now, that was exactly what she wanted.

EPILOGUE

I TOLD YOU I loved that doomed kind of love.

Who knew it could be this doomed?

People think Shakespeare said love is a many-splendored thing. But that was some other guy.

Shakespeare said it is merely a madness.

So where does the pendulum swing now?

Love, it turns out, is whatever it feels like being. It can be the grand gesture or the bad decision.

It can be a disaster, natural or human-made.

And, it seems, star-crossed lovers can come in threes. Destiny is cruel.

If Juliet learns Romeo's love was true, does it matter, given the circumstances?

If Romeo finally lets himself lose control for love, does it matter, if he doesn't survive the night?

Can they even have a moment, or will they be consumed by the flood, or the fire of passion?

Oh, and Jim. It seems what happens next will turn on him, doesn't it?

Tout est possible. . . .

You want to know more of what's next, do you? (Of course you do; I'm very good at this.)

Threats of death and deception aside (and I pass no judgments on which is worse), there's the small matter of a magazine.

Maintenant. A June issue. On the thin side. Usually not cause for much hubbub.

But in the layout featuring the model Gabrielle spreading her plumage all over Petite Asie, there just so happens to be something in the background that's causing waves:

Look closely and it appears to be none other than a Capulet (Juliet) and a Montague (Romeo) with fingertips touching.

Is it beneath me to say, *Oh, snap*? (Yes, that's more dated than calling me a bard.)

It appears, perhaps, that a certain couple forgot that all the world's a stage. And even when you think you're hidden, well, no.

Possibly it won't matter, with Juliet in the graveyard and Romeo potentially heading to one.

Maybe it's not them.

And the Templars are just a myth?

And James Redmond will "to be, not to be" and decide hostile takeovers aren't very nice?

And the course of true love runs smooth?

Alas . . . so many maybes.

Actually (and perhaps most surprising), that's all I can say for now.

ACKNOWLEDGMENTS

The authors would like to thank: Christy Ottaviano for her time, commitment, and vision; Fonda Snyder for her guardianship, care, and support; Jessica Anderson for keeping us on task and forward moving; Liz Dresner for her amazing artistry; Starr Baer for her careful attention and insight; Lauren Festa and Amanda Mustafic for being excited about our book and getting it in front of readers who will, we hope, love it.

Larry would also like to thank Victoria Lewis and Alex Cabral for enabling him to function.

We also thank our families, friends, and readers everywhere, without whom this book wouldn't be possible.

A SNEAK PEAK FROM BOOK 2 OF
THE ROMEO, JULIET AND JIM SERIES

THE HOTEL LEMIEUX had seen this kind of thing before. The walls had witnessed countless rendezvous, many of them best left behind with the threadbare sheets. Juliet knocked lightly on the door, seeing as it swung into the room that it had been left open for her. She hated the waiting and the secrecy. Or maybe she loved it, the way her pulse quickened when she saw his face. Whatever misgivings she had about subterfuge melted as he kissed her.

"Jim, I've missed you," Juliet said, using her foot to shut the door between them and the rest of the world. The lock clicked, and they were alone.

WE KNOW WE say Amor Vincit Omnia (Love Conquers All) . . . but will there be any survivors?